WHISPER
A
WARNING

WHISPER
A
WARNING

•

CHRISTINE BUSH

AVALON BOOKS
THOMAS BOUREGY AND COMPANY, INC.
401 LAFAYETTE STREET
NEW YORK, NEW YORK 10003

PRINTED IN THE UNITED STATES OF AMERICA
ON ACID-FREE PAPER
BY HADDON CRAFTSMEN, BLOOMSBURG, PENNSYLVANIA

This book is dedicated to my wonderful children, who constantly enrich my life: Abigail, Susannah, Maureen, Jacqueline and David. May you have love and laughter, health and happiness all of your days.

Chapter One

" "Yes! Yes! Yes!" Willow slammed the office phone into its cradle with gusto, then stood up and did a victory dance in the middle of the real estate office. Her exuberance didn't startle anyone. She plopped back into the chair, green eyes sparkling, and met the kindly brown eyes of the older man who sat behind her, tucked into the corner of the crammed room.

"Hey, Mr. Reynolds," she chirped, "it's the rock star from New York! He's going to see the White property at one this afternoon! 1.2 million dollars, here we go!"

"Go get 'em, Wilhemina Blake!" Mr. Reynolds said with an amused smile. "We could use a little cash influx into this place. Maybe we'll splurge. Since I'm making the coffee these days, I could go for a new coffeemaker. One of those newfangled Swedish jobs . . . this one is the pits."

He shrugged his shoulders at the aged coffeemaker that sat on the shelf beside him, pushing up his half-glasses at the same time, enjoying teasing Willow.

Willow pulled her five-foot, nine-inch frame out of the chair and stepped back to the gentle man who was her boss and the broker of the small real estate company. She bent over and kissed the top of his balding head, making him blush.

"Gee, Willow," he stammered, suddenly shuffling papers on his desk. "You're too much!"

"*You're* too much, Mr. Reynolds. But I'll tell you what.

1

When I clinch this deal, you and Mrs. Reynolds are going to take that second honeymoon trip to Sweden. You can pick up the coffeemaker while you're there.''

He was laughing now. ''Willow, the day you gave up coffee making and got your real estate license was a day for the record books. I'm better at taking care of the paperwork, and watching you guys sell! I'm also better at making coffee,'' he chided.

''True, all true,'' Willow conceded. ''Mildred,'' she said to the quiet woman who sat at the next desk. ''What kind of trouble are you up to today?''

Mildred looked up from her typewriter and blushed. She was ten years older than Willow's twenty-six years, and was almost the exact opposite of Willow's flamboyant style. Her straight brown hair was pulled back into a wooden barrette at the nape of her neck, and her face was scrubbed clean of any makeup or pretense. Her ''good sense'' white blouse was tied sedately in a bow at her neck.

''Showing houses,'' she spoke in her soft, airy voice. ''All day. I've got an appointment at eleven o'clock.''

The reference to time made Willow glance at the clock.

''Oh, gosh!'' Willow blurted, jumping to her feet. ''I'm due at the bank. I'm going to try to convince those financial felons to reconsider the rehab loan they turned down. These clients deserve that loan. It's just not fair. I'm going to put my two cents in to help them. It's the principle of the thing.''

Mr. Reynolds sighed and ran a hand through his hair. ''Life just isn't fair, is it? I wish I could help you. I wish I had the money to spare, Wilhelmina.''

''Don't waste a thought on it, Mr. R. The medical bills for Mrs. Reynolds are the important thing for you to worry about. We're going to keep breaking those sales records, and sooner or later, we'll all be able to *make* things more fair. Okay?''

"Okay, kiddo. Good luck at the bank, and good luck with the rock star. You *will* be back in time to meet with Manxo Manxo, right? I have to admit he intimidates me. It's like he's from another planet."

"Just sing him a few Frank Sinatra tunes if he beats me here. That will keep him quiet. Or ask him about politics. Now *that* ought to be a conversation."

"I have a feeling you'd better just be back in time."

"Gotcha."

When Mr. Reynolds had hired her a few short years before, he had seen something special in the tall lanky blond who had been valiantly trying to bluff her way into a job with absolutely no skills at all. She had been young, alone, and determined to support herself when she had arrived in town. He had instantly respected her spunk and drive. He hired her as his part-time receptionist on the spot. She had never let him down.

She had learned every facet of the real estate field, and when she had decided to earn her real estate license, he had been proud and supportive. And she had proved him right.

She packed her briefcase to make the short trip to the bank, taking a moment to check herself in her compact mirror. Today, her short blond hair was brushed back in a sophisticated style. Stately pearl earrings matched the band of pearls around her neck. She wore a touch of artistically applied makeup. She stared at herself for a moment, then nodded her head. She looked just right for the bank.

Tall and slim, she was wearing a pair of flowing wide-legged trousers, in a soft yellow rayon material, topped with a matching tunic. It was belted at the waist, and ended gently, far above her knees.

With her short blond hair and emerald green eyes, she looked like a breath of summer day, an exquisite burst of sunshine.

With a deep sigh, and a wave to Mr. Reynolds who was still on the phone, she stepped out into the June sunshine to face the bank. She flung her briefcase unceremoniously into her car, parked at the curb, a bright yellow convertible Miata, and folded her tall frame into the driver's seat.

The engine roared to life, and she pulled out into the traffic, heading for the bank. She was probably going to lose, she knew, but she would go down fighting. It was, as Mr. Reynolds had so perceptively understood, the principle of the thing.

June was supposed to be a beautiful month. It once had meant flowers, sunshine, and sweet-smelling women in airy dresses. But not anymore. Rockford Farquahar Harrison III sat leaning on his elbows, sitting at his well-polished cherry wood desk. The desk had a shine so bright he could almost see his reflection in it. Amazing, he thought, that he was sitting here just evaluating the shine from his desk.

He looked out the tall graceful windows of the law office, which once had been the mansion home of one of Ryerstown's founding citizens. He had a first-floor, corner office. Good light exposure. Beautiful hardwood floors peeked out from the edges of the tasteful Oriental carpet. The furniture was exquisite. The obligatory rows of legal books lined the walls behind his desk. He couldn't have cared less.

It was a lawyer's dream come true, this expansive, well-appointed office in this solid, trustworthy law firm owned by his uncle. A new town. A fresh start. He should feel happy; he should feel thankful, he chided himself. He wished he had been full of the usual optimism that had been a trademark in his early life.

But the fact was, he didn't feel anything. That youthful optimism had evaporated, gone like a puff of smoke, with one brutal gunshot. In its wake, it had left . . . nothing. He felt empty, drained, and tired of the phony smiling face he had worn for the past two weeks since he had arrived in town.

He felt like he was letting his sister Georgina down, letting himself down. But he seemed powerless to change it.

George was always consoling him, telling him to relax, just do his best, and let time take its course. But then, George had more patience and optimism than just about any living creature he had ever met.

"It is just grief," George said. "Put things in their right perspective, and you'll be able to find joy in life again."

He wasn't even that greedy. He'd settle for peace, or just a little happiness. He'd be delighted with a little hope, or enthusiasm.

But for now, he just had his work, so he stopped looking out the tall windows of the office, ignoring the busy small-town main street that paraded by, and turned his attention back to the legal work at his fingertips. Deftly pressing buttons on his desk equipment, he quickly dictated a few letters, then relayed the rough draft of a simple will for one of the firm's elderly clients. It was not mind-boggling stuff, certainly not the kind of law that he was used to practicing, but it kept him busy and held his attention; at least for a while.

But then, he was suddenly distracted by a distinctive flash of yellow from the sidewalk across the street. He raised his eyes and stared.

She was tall. Slim. She was very blond, with hair as short as her legs were long. She was wearing some kind of pants, mysterious, flowing things that alternately billowed and clung to her legs as she moved. He liked the way she walked, with long, deliberate steps, and an athletic, swingy gait. She wore a loose-fitting top of the same yellow color, and the effect was breathtaking. Eye-catching.

He found himself smiling for the first time in months as

he watched her climb into a sports car at the curb. A vision of yellow gold. Even the car matched! He was still staring openmouthed as the flash of yellow darted down the street. She was gone.

He felt a funny kind of loss, like a kid who was promised an ice cream sundae, and then didn't get it. He finally let his breath out, amazed that he had held it so long. His mind started ticking . . . who was she? Where did she come from? How would he find her again?

Within a minute or two, he had calmed himself down. The golden woman was gone, and he probably would never see her again, so that was that. But his strong reaction had produced one happy realization . . . he sure wasn't dead yet.

It was almost noon when Willow emerged from the bank. Perhaps it would be accurate to say that Willow exploded from the bank. She was in a rage. She stomped her feet all the way to her convertible.

"Of all the cruel, unfeeling people I have seen—" She flung her briefcase into the car, and this time, didn't hesitate the second it would take to open the door. She climbed right over the side of the car and plopped herself into the driver's seat.

"It's not fair . . . it's not right . . . it makes me so darn mad."

With the last three syllables, she pounded on the steering wheel, finally stopping because her hand felt burnt from the hot steering wheel that had been exposed to the sun.

She had failed at the bank. Logically, she had known before she had gone that she was chasing a rainbow, fighting a lost cause, but deep in her heart, she had hoped for a miracle. But when a bank didn't want to lend money, they simply didn't lend it. They could come up with a multitude of legal reasons to justify their decisions. Banks were like that. Powerful. And discriminatory. Just hiding their prejudices under a lot of financial jargon.

She took a deep breath, and focused on the car. The engine sprang to life, and she roared out of the parking lot, heading back toward the main street of town and her real estate office. Not only had they turned down her appeal, they had kept her waiting an extra forty minutes, so that now she was rushing against the clock for her afternoon appointment for the White property.

She pulled up to the curb, thankful that her usual space was available. This time, she was calm enough to open the car door, and exited the vehicle with a lot more decorum than when she had entered. Decorum. She tended to forget about that when she was mad. Wait until Mr. Reynolds heard about her behavior at the bank!

She opened the heavy door, and found the office was empty, except for Mr. Reynolds, who was sitting at his desk, munching on a salad.

"Sit down, Wilhemina," he said between chews. "Calm down. The bank called, so I know it didn't go well."

"The bank called you already?" It was worse than she thought.

"Seemed they thought I should know that one of my realtors stood up on her chair at the conference table and started reciting the Constitutional amendments pertaining to discrimination at the top of her voice."

"I was a little . . . mad. They were so staid—so self-righteous." She winced. "But maybe that was too much, standing up on the chair and all. Sorry for embarrassing you. It didn't do any good anyway."

"But did you feel like you said your piece?" His old eyes twinkled.

"I felt like Patrick Henry."

"Well then, good for you, Wilhemina. You always follow your heart, and that's okay. You gained one supporter, by the way. Did you notice the nun who was at the meeting? She also called and said to congratulate you for your 'spine.' Seems to think that there aren't too many people with a 'spine' in this town, and she was glad to see one in action. It was probably worth scuffing a chair, Wilhemina.''

She smiled. ''Do you know, Mr. Reynolds,'' she said thoughtfully as she plopped into her desk chair, throwing one leg casually over the arm of the seat, ''that you are the only person in the entire world who can call me Wilhemina and get away with it?''

''Too bad. Wilhemina is a pretty name.''

''Don't spread it around, Mr. R. Remember my famous temper. Willow is just fine.''

She told him about the bank. Earlier in the year, she had assisted an organization in purchasing a property to be used as a group home for AIDS patients. They had won the battle of getting community acceptance and support. But recently, the group had applied for a rehab loan to make necessary improvements to the property. The loan had been rejected.

''We'll have to find another way,'' she concluded, ''but right now, I've got to get ready for Manxo Manxo.''

Mr. Reynolds laughed and shook his head.

She grabbed a small tote bag that she kept under her desk, and disappeared into the ladies' room. Hair, makeup, shoes, jewelry—they all had to go. In minutes, she emerged.

Her eyes were made up much darker now. Large gold hoops hung from her ears, and around her neck were several strands of gold chain. Hair mousse had given her short hair a slightly spiky look, and the golden sash that she had worn around her waist was now tied around her head as a headband, its tails hanging down her back. The yellow tunic, unbelted now, had become a very short dress. The pants were gone. Long, tanned legs were set off by a pair of golden espadrille shoes, their long ties crisscrossing up her legs and tying behind the knee.

"I don't believe it," exclaimed Mr. Reynolds, as he got a look at her. "You have done many weird things, but this is one of the highest on the list. You look like you just stepped out of an L.A. nightclub."

"Good. That's what I was hoping for. Flashy and wild, that's what Manxo likes, according to his agent on the phone. I'm going to clinch this deal, Mr. R."

He shook his head in wonder. "If your method works, it works. But I think Willow herself, without the getup, is still good enough. Just be careful."

She stuck a mobile phone in her pocketbook. "Call me if you need me," she called gaily, waving with a flourish as she stepped out the door. A long white limo with black-tinted glass was just pulling to the curb. She put on a wide smile and greeted the face that was familiar to her from album covers and CD labels.

"Manxo," she exclaimed. "You've going to *love* this property, and it's such a steal. . . ." The rock star took one look at her, and his face lit up.

"We'll have to take the limo, unless you want to dump the suit." She motioned to the dark-suited agent in the backseat. "My sports car only has two seats," she gushed, her long legs climbing into the limo, Manxo's low voice answering in agreement. The limo door swung shut and the vehicle left the curb.

Mr. Reynolds watched from the window and shook his head. Too much spunk for her own good. He wished she wasn't so alone. But she'd probably make the deal, if he knew Willow. And if, by any stretch of the imagination, the deal wasn't right, she'd probably come back with a contract to sing backup on Manxo's next album instead— that was Willow!

Chapter Two

The afternoon, for once, flew by quickly in the law office. Rockford kept his mind on his work and had sorted through and settled a lot of paperwork by the time it was time to quit for the day. His mind had strayed a few times to the amazing blond he had seen from the window, but his well-practiced self-discipline brought him back to his task.

The phones had stopped ringing; the last clients could be heard passing in the hallway on their way to the door. The staff in his Uncle William's firm seemed competent and friendly, but basically they had left him alone since his arrival, sensing his aloofness, and giving him time to settle in.

He suspected William had briefed them on the tragedy that had resulted in his leaving his father's firm and his career in criminal law.

When his uncle had benevolently offered him a job in his firm, he hadn't been able to come up with a reason to turn it down. The offer had actually been his sister Georgina's idea, he was sure. Knowing George's amazing ways, it wasn't much of a surprise that William had taken her up on the suggestion. One didn't cross George and come out unscathed, in a manner of speaking.

It wasn't that George was violent . . . she was absolutely not. She was *tenacious*. Like a pit bull. Or like one of those flies that buzzes around your head, not biting or stinging or even landing, but driving you mad nonetheless. If you

10

wanted to keep George from buzzing, you did what she said. Case closed.

The rest of the family had about given up on him. He had left the firm, which was considered a breach on its own accord. But then he had persisted in sitting around and doing *nothing*. Doing nothing was not acceptable to the Harrison heritage. One might not work for money, like his mother, the queen of charities, but one worked. One achieved.

But he had been, he could see now, in a deep depression, unable to cope with the grief and guilt and pain of his friend Peter's death. No one had been willing to talk about that. No one understood. Except George.

Georgina Canfield Harrison had been born a few short years after he had made his appearance in the world. She had always had a certain sense of maturity and wisdom that never seemed to fit her tiny elflike appearance. She had deemed herself ''George'' from an early age, and no one had bothered to fight with her about it. It was understood that you wouldn't win anyway. George was George.

But not only was George his sister, she also *was* a sister. Sister George. George had entered the convent the very day she had graduated from Smith College, and she had happily been a nun ever since. She was a member of a progressive community, where the members were assigned to serve in a parish but were encouraged to live on their own in the community they served. George lived in Ryerstown, Pennsylvania, in a simple but spacious apartment on the second floor of a glorious old Victorian home.

When she had decided that her brother Rockford needed to be shaken out of his lethargy, she had contacted the uncle who lived in her town, and had started the ball rolling. She had invited Rockford to visit her, and when he had complied, she had literally kidnapped him, and coerced him into studying for the Pennsylvania bar exam. Buzz buzz. Not in the mood to argue, he had followed her well-thought-out directions and suggestions, and had passed the exam with flying colors.

So now he was ensconced in Uncle William's firm, still living with George, and gradually feeling the smoky haze of depression that had hovered over him begin to dissipate.

"Things will get better. Just give yourself time." Thank goodness for George. She had been his anchor, his bossy guiding light. So his life was slowly cranking up again, one full year since Peter's death.

He could remember the day as if it had happened just yesterday. He had planned to meet Peter for lunch at the prestigious Winchester Club, known for its sedate elegance and 120-year-old history of gracious service to New York's elite. When Rockford was shown to his usual table, Peter was already seated, the chilled bottle of wine ready to pour, strains of Mozart in the air.

"You beat me but good, you smooth talker." There was a hint of criticism in Peter's voice. "Sit down and celebrate. The scum went free."

Rockford grinned, his adrenaline still pumping. He liked to win. "Poor loser, Emerson? Forget your lines in the closing statement? Maybe the jury didn't like your tie, ever think of that?" He squinted his eyes at his tablemate critically. "Come to think of it, I'm not too overly fond of that tie myself!"

They shook hands, smiling, settling at the table.

Rockford had been born to money and power. Peter was self-made, and liked to describe himself as hardworking and principled. Rockford described him as hardheaded.

Their friendship had been forged at college, then at Harvard Law School. At graduation, Rockford had comfortably settled into the corner office of his father's prestigious law firm, Harrison, Hasbrough and Jacobs. He had expected

Peter to come along. The firm had been more than willing. Peter had not.

Instead, Peter had opted for lower pay and grueling hours as an assistant district attorney for the city of New York, a crusader for justice, law, and order. He didn't like to lose in court like he had today.

"I thought I had him, big shot," Peter said over the rim of his wineglass. "Evidence, brilliant final argument . . . to say nothing of the fact that the guy was absolutely dead guilty."

Rockford looked pensively at his friend. He had been surprised with the jury's verdict himself. His defense had been stellar. His client, he was pretty sure, was far from it.

They had met in court before, though with the size of the New York court system, the odds were such that it didn't happen often. On the rare occasion that they met in court, they had an ironclad rule. They would ethically keep their distance during the course of the trial, then meet here at the club for lunch after the verdict, and the winner would pay. So far, it had kept their friendship intact.

"I didn't like this case a bit, Pete," Rockford admitted quietly. Waiters buzzed busily but unobtrusively around them. "I did what I was hired to do, but I didn't have a lot of faith in the guy."

Peter wasn't smiling. "You're too smart to have faith in the guy. Marco Slergetti is a first-degree creep. He was guilty. I've got to admit that it sticks in my craw, buddy, that you'd defend somebody who was guilty of killing an old lady like that."

"A jury of twelve didn't convict him, Peter."

"A jury of twelve believed in the defense counsel. They believed that you believed in your client. They believed *you*."

"Whoa, man, what's gotten into you? It's not like we

haven't both won or lost cases to each other before. What's this all about?''

Peter's face looked tight and drawn.

"We both lose here, Rock. You can't tell me that you're happy about defending a guy like that, knowing that he would be out on the streets again, killing someone else. It's like your heart is dead. Where's your sense of honor? Is it the money? You've got enough, man. Don't put a price on your integrity."

"A man is entitled to a defense."

"Spare me. Sooner or later, you're going to have to realize that there's more to law than winning or losing. It's not like a soccer game, Rock. People's lives are at stake here. Tell me honestly, did you think the guy was innocent? He's the head of a mob family. He orders hits the way you order lunch. Did you think even for a moment about the fact that you might not want to defend him, that you had a choice? Or do you just put yourself on stage and do your father's bidding? What's it going to take to wake you up, Rock?''

Rockford's throat felt tight. Peter's eyes burned into his. "I didn't think. I took the case, and I wanted to win. I won."

Peter shook his head. "You should have turned the case down, Rockford. You didn't win. You lost. You lost your integrity. Cheers."

With sad eyes, Peter lifted his glass in a mock salute. Rockford stared at him, his words stinging like barbs. Not too many people on this earth dared to criticize Rockford Farquahar Harrison III. But he knew that Peter was right. He had only wanted to win. He had disliked the client intensely, and he had, as Peter had charged, suspected that his client was guilty of the heinous crime as charged.

But he had wanted to win. So he hadn't asked the tough questions, and he had ignored the nagging burr-under-the-saddle feeling he had been having that his life wasn't going the way it should. His ethical, pain-in-the-neck friend Peter was right.

But before he could speak, a white-jacketed waiter moved beside him. In a split second, Rockford's eye registered the gun raised in his left hand, aimed directly at Peter. The gun blasted, hitting his friend squarely in the chest.

"That's from Marco," the man hissed in a gravelly voice, as he spun on his heel and ran.

Pandemonium broke out. Rockford sat rooted in his chair, frozen to the spot. People screamed and scrambled around him.

Broken, he sat across the white linen-clad table from Peter. His friend had died instantly. The light in his eyes had been extinguished like a blown-out candle with the impact. Rockford watched the giant red splotch on Peter's chest grow larger, soaking his tie as he sprawled back in his chair.

Mozart still played in the background, but it was almost drowned out by the sound of nearing police sirens.

Peter was dead, and he felt more responsible than if he had been the one who pulled the trigger. Marco. Peter had said that he would murder again. Peter had been right. And Rockford Farquahar Harrison III had set him free to order it.

Paramedics had arrived, loading the body onto a stretcher to be taken to the hospital. Death would simply not be pronounced at the Winchester Club. It just wasn't done.

One of "New York's Finest" was shooting questions at him, and he answered automatically, his mind disengaged, his eyes still seeing the horror of the blood-soaked tie of his best friend.

The gunman had been shot on the sidewalk, outside the club. An APB went out for Marco Slergetti, but he was not found. It was suspected that he had already left the country under an assumed name.

After the funeral, Rockford had handed in his resignation from the family firm, despite his father's strong objections.

He didn't know quite what he was going to do with his life, but one thing he knew for sure. Peter had been right. There had been no winners at that fatal trial. No winners at all.

He sat in the empty silence for a minute. Down the hall a door slammed, bringing him back to the present. He pushed the memories away.

Everyone had finished their day of work, leaving for the second part of their lives, to see spouses, friends, lovers. He hated this time of the day, when he would have to face the facts of his empty life, with no one to go home to.

George, of course, would blow in sooner or later, revved up about some cause she was attending to, and then usually blow back out again. But for him, Rockford Farquahar Harrison III, former dazzle boy of New York City, he was looking at a night consisting of a lonely dinner followed by TV reruns.

He looked out the window before rising to put on his suit coat. A long white stretch limo was pulling up to the curb across the street. He decided he should look out of the window more often. There was more excitement in Ryerstown than he had originally believed.

The doors of the limo opened, and two people got out. He rubbed his eyes. He could have sworn it was Manxo Manxo, a top-of-the-charts rock star who crooned wild love songs with a vibrant beat. He had seen him once or twice in the posh New York nightclubs he had frequented in the past. What was he doing in Ryerstown? He forgot the question, however, as the next passenger came into view. It was a tall, leggy blond, a real eye-catcher. Not at all like his leggy blond from the afternoon, but beautiful nonetheless. He watched for a minute, laughing at himself. He was turning into a voyeur.

From her wild spiked hair, to her funny, strappy shoes that crisscrossed up miles of bare leg, she took his breath away. Her face was almost hidden behind an enormous pair of dark sunglasses, and big, golden hoops sparkled in her ears.

The two disappeared into a small real estate office across the street. Maybe the rocker and his girlfriend were buying some local property. That would be big news in Ryerstown!

He left the window when they disappeared from sight, finally leaving the quiet office and locking the door behind him. The sun was still high in the June sky, even though it was past 5:00 P.M. There were still many hours to kill before the night really arrived and the day was officially over.

Rockford sighed, and headed home.

Chapter Three

"Congratulations, Willow!" "Atta girl!" The office was charged with energy after Manxo Manxo's long gleaming limo had pulled away from the curb, carrying the famous singer who was now the proud owner of a 1.2 million-dollar property. Clutching his accepted agreement of sale, Manxo (who Willow had decided was really quite a nice guy) had gone back to the city to arrange the financing for his new country estate.

"This is the biggest sale we've ever had, Willow," said Mr. Reynolds quietly, as he sat reviewing the papers in awe. The final closing on the property would take place in two weeks' time. "What a commission!"

"Book the trip, Mr. R." she said, handing him a brochure of tours of Sweden and Scandinavia she had stopped to pick up at the local travel agency. "I wasn't kidding. Take Mrs. Reynolds on that trip we talked about."

He clutched the brochure and chuckled. "I *am* going to take her, Wilhemina. I'm going to call and make the reservation right now. I just hope her heart can take the shock!"

Willow's eyes shined with emotion, but she blinked back the tears. Crying wasn't something she had in her repertoire. Willow Blake did not cry.

She swung around and plunked herself down at her desk. "Make sure you get the coffeemaker, now. We're counting on you!"

Even Mildred chuckled.

Willow closed up her desk for the day, pleased with the outcome of the sale, and feeling the warmth of the people she worked with. The money would come in handy to keep her life plugging along. She'd pay her back bills, put away a financial buffer, and still have money left to start a rehab fund for the group in the AIDS home. She'd failed at the bank, but she wouldn't fail the boys. Already her mind was brainstorming gimmicks to encourage the community to donate the necessary funds. She felt good.

She headed for home, letting the wind whip her still-moussed hair in the Miata, pulling down the long drive to her cottage in a few short minutes. Energized by the sight of her simple but peaceful place, settled on the back of an old horse farm, she climbed out of the car, stretching her long legs and happy to be home. Her big orange cat came to greet her, with a small black kitten in tow.

She jumped into the shower, washing the last traces of makeup from her face and mousse from her hair, and climbed into a pair of well-worn jeans and cowboy boots. She pulled an oversized Yale sweatshirt over her head, and towel-dried her hair. It was time to go meet the kids.

Willow had moved into her little cottage a year ago, when it had become available, but she had been living in a small room at the farm since the day she had stepped off the bus with no more than a backpack on her back. At seventeen, taking all the courage she had possessed, she had left her cruel and destructive father for a fresh start at life.

The bus had left Philadelphia and headed for the sprawling suburbs. She had been seated next to a cute little girl who was traveling alone, about eight years old. Her legs, below her knees, wore heavy metal braces.

It had really been Maybeth who had introduced her to Higher Horizons Farm. ''I'm going to a really cool farm,'' she had said with a giggle. "You go horseback riding there. I'm going to learn how to ride a horse. Like in the movies."

Willow had been charmed with her effervescent personality, but skeptical about her plans.

"Is somebody meeting you? Have you done this before?"

"Miss Maggie will fetch me, Mom says. My teacher got it all fixed up. Mom couldn't come 'cause we only had money for one bus fare. But that's all right, 'cause Miss Maggie will be there to take me to the farm. Then I'll ride my horse."

Willow had looked down at the braces, praying the little girl's hopes wouldn't be dashed by reality. She knew just how dashing reality could be. She still had bruises on her arm to remind her.

So she had followed Maybeth off the bus in Ryerstown, determined that her dreams would not be squashed by the unknown "Maggie."

Maybeth had maneuvered herself off the high bus steps, refusing the help that Willow offered.

"Thanks, ma'am," she had shyly said. "But I can do this. Just watch." And she could.

And then there was Miss Maggie. Maggie McCann, a five-foot, eleven-inch, gray-haired ball of energy, had looked much less than her sixty years as her face had exploded in a smile for Maybeth as the youngster had struggled off the bus.

"That was real good, Maybeth," she said in the quiet, steady voice that Willow later had learned to love. "Ready to meet your horse?"

Willow had tears in her eyes watching the excited girl.

"How about you, Blondie?" Maggie had drawled. "You here with Maybeth? I thought she was coming alone."

"I, uh, met her on the bus. I was . . . concerned."

Maggie nodded. "You late for something? In a rush?"

Willow shook her head.

"You want to come meet a horse, too? You look like you could use a friend to talk to. Horses listen real good . . . and I can always use a hand." Maggie knew a runaway when she saw one.

So she had been bundled along, backpack over her shoulder, and she had ridden out to Higher Horizons Farm with Maggie and Maybeth in the ancient Suburban that she had used forever to tote kids and horse supplies.

She had fallen in love for the first time that day. With Maybeth, Maggie, Higher Horizons Farm, and with a horse named Mac. She had watched in astounded awe as Maggie had worked with the vivacious little girl, strapping her into a special equestrian saddle to keep her weakened legs secure on the horse. She had seen the esteem climb higher and higher as the little girl experienced the magic of horseback riding.

First working with Maggie until she felt secure, Maybeth ended the session in the ring with four other physically challenged kids. Maggie sat on a tall stool in the center of the ring, giving lesson commands and evaluating each student. Teenaged volunteers were assigned to assist each rider. Willow was mesmerized.

She had mucked stalls, and learned about horses. She had been standing, hot and sweaty, with pieces of hay stuck in her long blond hair, when she turned and found Maggie standing watching her. Her long arms folded in front of her, she leaned one hip against the beam of the stall.

"You did good work, Wilhelmina. Thank you." Willow took the twenty-dollar bill that Maggie had offered, dreaming of dinner.

"It was fantastic. Unbelievable. I loved seeing this."

"I'm going to take Maybeth to the bus. Her mom will be waiting for her at the other end. You want a ride?"

She had felt quietly desperate on the ride to the bus. For

the second time that day, she had mustered the courage to make a change in her life. "I, um, don't have to rush anywhere, Maggie. Any chance you need help at the barn tomorrow?"

Maggie smiled with understanding. "You on your own, Wilhemina?

Wilhemina felt filled with shame. "Yes, ma'am."

"Well, pick up your shoulders and stand proud, then. Don't do no good to hang around like a dog who's been kicked. You're a good worker, and you like kids. If you want to put some time in at the barn, that's okay with me. I don't pay much, but you could have a room at the farm, and give me a hand with the kids and the horses when you can. Then you could get a part-time job in town maybe."

They had made a deal.

"Funny, I shouldn't call you Blondie, but Wilhemina doesn't suit you. People's names usually fit."

"I hate my name."

"What would you call yourself?"

"I don't know. Maybe Willow. That sounds better."

"Sounds fine. Like a tall graceful tree. Now that suits. So call yourself Willow."

"Just like that? Change my name?"

"Why not? A person has to like the things about themselves, that's the most important thing. We have a responsibility to be the best we can be, and to do whatever it takes to get us there."

It had been her first lesson in personal empowerment, the first time she had felt that she could make positive changes in her life. She had felt like a burst of sunshine had descended upon her dark thoughts and fears and shame, pushing them away.

Willow was born, and she had Maggie's insight to thank for it.

That had been almost nine years before. Then she had

met Mr. Reynolds, and began to learn about real estate. But she had still spent time with Maggie and the horse barn and her special kids for part of every day.

Glancing at the clock, she quickly set out two bowls of cat food, grabbed an apple from the round kitchen table in her cottage, and shut the cottage door behind her, as she jogged the short distance to the barn that was her second home.

Chapter Four

"You want to take in a movie, George?" Rockford put the question forth speculatively, though he could predict his sister's response. She had just come home, had eaten a giant sandwich, and was scurrying around the kitchen.

"I've got to go over to the church. Choir practice. You want to come?"

He laughed. It was a standing joke between them. George was always trying to get him involved in life, and he was always resisting.

"You ought to do something, though, other than sit around this place and watch commercials. Your brain is going to turn to mush. Go to the mall and watch people. Or go to the library."

She was gathering a large stack of sheet music, and putting on her coat at the same time. It always amazed him, how George would always do more than one thing at a time. "Saves time," she always said.

"Okay, okay, don't lecture. Message received."

"You have to get involved in life, Rockford. Do some good for somebody. Like this girl I saw today."

"I saw a girl today, too, by the way. Gorgeous. A heart-stopper."

"I'm not talking about hormones, you animal. I'm talking about commitment. About passion. There was this girl at the bank, and she was fighting to get a loan approved for the people who have started the AIDS home. You know, the guys I have been working with through the hospital program.''

''You'll have to forgive me for forgetting. I have a little trouble keeping all your causes straight.''

''That's because you're not paying attention. You're focused on *you*, instead of the world.'' He took the criticism because he knew it came from love. He also knew it was probably true, and had the grace to feel slightly uncomfortable.

''So what about the girl. Does she live in the house?''

''No, she's the realtor who helped them qualify for the house. She just felt like they weren't getting a fair shake, and she wanted to do something about it. It was beautiful, inspiring!''

''So what did she do?''

''She stood up on her chair and started spouting the Bill of Rights from the Constitution. A crusader for human rights. Really, it was quite inspirational.''

George had managed to get her coat on, and partly buttoned, still holding the stack of music. Rockford stepped over, gently finishing her buttons, and then tapped her on the chin.

''So they got the loan?''

''Nope. They got turned down flat.''

''So what's the point? Where's the inspiration in that?''

''You still don't get it, big brother. But I'm not going to give up on you. It's the principle of the thing. You have to stand up for what you believe in, for what you want, even if you fail. It's the *principle* of the thing.''

Suddenly, Rockford was transported back to the moment in the restaurant with Peter, hearing his best friend in the world say the same words. *''It's the principle of the thing. . . . Don't lose your integrity. . . .''*

His mouth felt dry, and his heart started to hammer. With

his eyes closed, he could see Peter's strong-willed face, clear as day.

George put down the music and wrapped her arms around him. She had seen this reaction before.

"Maybe you've got to take a positive step, Rockford. Instead of feeling guilty that Peter's dead, maybe you could do something in his honor, something that he would be proud of."

He pulled back and looked at George, feeling balanced again. "Why do I think you have a plan here?"

She grinned. "I can see it now—The Peter A. Benson Endowment Fund. You have money to spare, Mr. Big Shot. You could start a fund to help worthy causes in Peter's name. Just think of how much he would love that! You could start with the Ryerstown AIDS Home, Rockford. You could make a difference, and then people like that fantastic girl today might be able to make a dent in society."

She gathered everything up again, and sped for the door, not even giving him time to talk. Warp speed, that was George.

" 'Bye," she shouted over her shoulder as she went out the door. "Just think about it. I love you."

"I love you, too, Sister George," he said softly, knowing that she wouldn't hear him, because she was already gone, headed for her next cause.

When the evening lesson at the barn had finished, Willow headed into town to the library.

"We'll have a new rider in the Physically Handicapped Teens class tomorrow night," Maggie had told her. "She is severely epileptic, and is suffering from bouts of depression from the many limitations in her life."

Willow wanted to do some research about epilepsy before meeting the girl. With limited time before the library's closing, she didn't waste a minute, jumping into her car and pulling into the library lot quickly. The library was bustling. She knew the location of the medical research section because she had used it several times before. She browsed through several titles on the shelf.

Rockford had taken George's advice. Not feeling like dealing with the crowds and noise at the mall, he had gone to the library. After wandering around for a while, he had started thinking about the other things that George had said. Was he really that self-involved? The answer made him feel very uncomfortable. He needed to think that through, to make a change.

George's idea about the fund in Peter's name was an intriguing one. She had hit the nail right on the proverbial head. Peter would have loved the idea. He found himself in the medical research section of the library, looking up information on AIDS.

He was sitting at a table, reading a rather lengthy and wordy article in a medical journal, when he was distracted by a pair of legs. A long pair of legs, they were not clearly visible, because the owner of the legs was standing on the other side of the tall bookshelf he was facing.

The bookshelves were not totally filled; in almost every row there were empty spaces that served almost as windows, peeking through to the next aisle.

The legs were wearing jeans, and the owner of said legs was moving slowly and gracefully along the aisle, moving in and out of view as she read the books on the shelf. He couldn't see the face, just the legs. But that was enough. The legs were just too intriguing. For the second time that day, he felt alive. Curiosity overcame him, and he got up from his chair to investigate the cause of his reaction. She had left the aisle, so he began cautiously strolling around the library . . . looking for a pair of legs. Amazing but true.

He found her. She was in the checkout line, holding a large book in one hand, a library card in the other. She was really tall, and gracefully thin, with short blond hair that was mussed and scattered. She wore jeans that hugged her long legs like a second skin, a pair of cowboy boots, and a large gray sweatshirt.

She looked comfortable, unpretentious, adorable. She also looked familiar. Was this the golden girl of the morning? Was this the sophisticated, well-dressed woman who had roared away in a yellow sports car, taking his heart right along with her? Style-wise, she looked totally different. But he knew . . . this was his golden girl, and he wasn't going to lose her again.

He could hear his pulse hammering in his ears, amazed that the people standing in line couldn't hear it in the quiet of the library. There were two people in back of her by the time he stepped into line, still holding his book on AIDS.

There was a teenage boy in line in front of her. He had asked a question of the myopic-looking clerk who was sitting at the checkout desk.

"Why are you bothering me, young man?" the clerk said in a nasty voice. "Can I help it if you can't find the book you're looking for? Don't you know the Dewey Decimal system? Just look at the numbers. Any idiot can do it. Go!" He waved the boy away with an impatient gesture. "Go look yourself. I've got to take care of these books." Rockford felt anger rising inside of him.

He saw the boy hang his head, embarrassed and frustrated. He walked dejectedly to the aisle the man had pointed toward.

Bang! Suddenly, there was a loud noise, and his attention was riveted once more to the desk, and the blond he had been following.

She had taken the large volume she had been carrying, and had smacked it down on the desk with all her might.

The crack resounded in the quiet library, and made everyone look her way.

"Just who do you think you are, Buster?" she said in a loud voice to the clerk. "Talking to a kid like that? This is a library, for Pete's sake. People come here for information, and you are supposed to provide it. Your salary is paid by taxpayers in this community, and that kid is a citizen here. You are out of line, buddy, and you ought to apologize and go help that kid."

"I have a job to do, young lady. My job is books. Books. You see these books here?" He gestured to the line of people who were waiting to check out books. "First I have to check out all these books. Then"—he gestured to the return desk by the door, which had piles of books on it— "I have to check all those back in, and put them back on the shelf. Books are my job. Not people." He smirked at her.

"You could have given that kid some quick advice instead of calling him names. It wouldn't have taken you a split second. You're a bully. I don't like bullies."

She left the line then, following the direction the young boy had gone. Rockford slipped out of line and followed her, intrigued.

"Hey," she said softly to the young boy who was struggling to find the book he was looking for. "Can I help?" He looked at her with thankful eyes, his misery apparent.

"I'm looking for this book on the Civil War. I've got a paper due tomorrow. I guess I really am an idiot. I can't seem to find it."

Willow smiled, and ruffled his dark hair. "Sure you can." She gave a few quick instructions, explaining the Dewey Decimal system, and how it worked. He listened attentively, then followed her directions. He found the book.

"Thanks, lady," he said, though the hurt was still hovering in his eyes.

"Willow. My name is Willow. What's yours?"

"Frank."

"Well, Frank, that bozo there just has a big abusive mouth. Don't buy into it. You're okay."

She looked thoughtful, still angry with the way the boy had been treated, and wishing there was a way to make a point. It came to her in a rush. "You want to get a little comical revenge?"

Frank nodded, the first time a smile etched itself on his face.

"Get out your library card, and follow me! The man loves books, we'll give him books."

Rockford followed the two as they sped around the library, trying to see what they were doing. It didn't make sense.

Within a few minutes, each of them had a giant stack of books, all large and heavy, and all selected from different secions of the library.

"Ten's the limit," Willow puffed under her load. "Put the one for your report on the top."

They moved to the checkout line and waited patiently. Several people who had been present during the incident with the clerk watched thoughtfully. Willow put her stack on the desk, and handed over her card.

"You're taking all these out?" He looked skeptical, but she didn't say a word. He checked out each book. "Thank you," she said in a loud voice. She stood to the side, waiting for her cohort. Rockford watched curiously, along with about a dozen other people who had watched the clerk in action.

Frank was next in line. The clerk looked nervous. He checked out the giant stack of books carefully. When he was finished, Frank picked up his stack and followed

Willow. She walked to the return desk, and plopped the entire pile onto the stacks waiting to be checked in, taking only her book on epilepsy off the top. Frank followed suit.

"Hey, you two," the clerk called out. "You can't do that, check out all those books, and then turn them right back in."

"And why is that? Is there a rule about that?" Willow pulled herself up to her full height, standing regally by the door.

The clerk bit his lip.

"We're speed readers, sir," she said with a broad smile. "But don't concern yourself with us. After all, you only want to be concerned with books. So here's a few more books to be concerned with. Have fun putting them away. It's not nice to bully people."

She stuck out her hand to Frank for a handshake, and the two headed for the door. "Feeling better, partner?" she said to the teenager.

"Absolutely. You were awesome."

"You're going to be pretty awesome yourself. You just had a lesson in personal empowerment, kiddo. Stand up for what you believe in. It's the principle of the thing!"

Rockford had stopped in his tracks, startled. The girl was outrageous; the girl was gorgeous. His golden girl had a heart of gold, too. The thought made him warm inside.

He sneaked a peek at the checkout line as he left the library. Four more people were standing there holding a mountain of books, joining in the protest. He smiled. The library clerk would think twice before being rude again— that is, if he ever got all those books put away!

He headed for his car, seeing the taillights of the yellow Miata speeding out the library lot. But he wasn't worried. He'd find her. He had to. She had stolen his heart.

Chapter Five

Mr. and Mrs. Reynolds left on their celebration trip to Sweden and Scandinavia on Monday, a week later. The office threw a bon voyage party for them, complete with a liberal sprinkling of confetti to cheer them as they took off in an airport limousine.

After the party, Willow was alone in the office, cleaning up the mess they'd made, and covering the phones. Mildred was out showing a property. They had hired a temporary worker to manage the telephones in Mr. Reynolds's absence, but the woman wouldn't start until the next day.

Willow was on one phone line, answering questions about a house that they had advertised for sale over the weekend, when the second line rang insistently. She put the first call on hold to pick up the line.

"Reynolds Real Estate, Willow speaking. How can I help you?"

"I got a property I want to put a bid in on. Can you help me with that?"

"Sure. I'd love to. But can I call you right back? I have someone on the other line. Just give me your number. . . ."

"Never mind. I'll call back." *Click.*

The connection was broken. The caller had hung up.

Willow sighed. It wasn't the first rude phone call she had ever received. She quickly clicked over to her original customer, and jumped back into her conversation about the advertised property. Setting up an afternoon appointment to show it, she took the necessary information from the potential buyer, and logged the time in her book, before hanging up.

The phone rang again immediately.

"I called before. I want to buy a property."

"Which property were you interested in, sir? Did you want to make an appointment to see it?"

"No appointment. I just want to buy it. You talk to the owner, and set it up." The man sounded very gruff.

Willow felt the stirrings of apprehension.

"Is the property listed with our office, sir? Or someone else's?"

"It's not listed. I want you to make an offer to the owner, an enticement to get them to sell."

"I see. And your name is . . ."

"Charley. Charley Morse."

"Well, Mr. Morse, how about coming in and meeting with me about the property in question. It's not the usual way we do real estate business here, but I'm willing to hear you out and approach the owner. We could propose the price, and it could be presented along with your financial qualifications. . . ."

"Listen, lady, I don't intend to get involved in any penny-ante meetings with you or with anybody else. The property is on Old Silo Road; it's a farm owned by a couple named Burdett. I'm offering half a million dollars, and I want the deal done quick. Cash. Pronto."

Willow was familiar with the property he was naming. It was a short way down the road from Higher Horizons Farm. The Burdetts were an older couple, and the small ten-acre farm had lain fallow for years. The house was an old clapboard in need of repair, and the barn had seen better days.

"You're willing to pay five hundred thousand dollars for the Burdett place?" she asked incredulously.

"You got a major problem with that, lady?"

She decided she couldn't stand the guy. "Let's say that first I have a major problem with being called 'lady' in that tone of voice. Use it again, and I'll hang up the phone."

The man chuckled. "A touchy one. Sorry. Check out the property and see if the Burdetts will sell. If they say yes, I'll be in tomorrow to sign all the paperwork."

With a loud click, the phone went dead again. Charley Morse needed a crash course in telephone manners. Willow sat for a minute drumming her fingers on the desk. Half a million in cash? It was an unorthodox way to do business, and the man gave her the chills.

But half a million! Think of what the Burdetts could do with money like that! And quite honestly, think of what she could do with another choice commission this month. . . . It wouldn't hurt to ride out to the Burdetts' farm and toss the idea around. She'd be honest, and tell them she had no credentials on the buyer yet, that it could even be a hoax. But half a million dollars . . . She thought they deserved to know.

She tried to call the farm, but their number was unlisted. She decided to drop by to see them, as soon as Mildred returned from her showing. She didn't like the man, but business was business. And he had certainly piqued her curiosity with his outlandish bid.

It was late afternoon by the time she pulled her Miata down the rocky drive that led to the Burdett farm. The car bounced along the rutted road as she tried to avoid the tangled bushes that had overgrown their space on the side of the drive, encroaching on the right of way with their overgrown greenery. The farm road was certainly in disrepair.

She could see the Burdetts' pickup truck parked next to the farmhouse. She parked alongside of it, climbing carefully up the worn wooden steps to the porch. Although showing the signs of age, the house was neat and clean, and had a well-loved look. The front door was open, letting in the fresh summer air. She peered through the aged screen door, hearing sounds from the back of the house.

"Mrs. Burdett? Mr. Burdett? Are you home?"

"Well, it's Willow from Maggie's," called Mrs. Burdett back over her shoulder as she crossed the hallway to let Willow in. "Herbert, come here and say hello."

Willow grinned at the elderly couple who came to greet her. Mr. Burdett wore a well-used pair of overalls and a scuffed pair of barn boots. Mrs. Burdett was wrapped in a faded gingham apron, covering her jeans and sweatshirt. Both had short gray curly hair, and wore big smiles.

"Come in and sit." Mrs. Burdett gestured toward the kitchen. "We're delighted to have company. We just cleaned up from lunch. Is everything all right with Maggie and the children?"

Willow sat at the comfortable kitchen table, sipping a cup of tea, and munching on homemade muffins. "Maggie and the kids are great. I'm here on a different kind of business. Did you know I'm a realtor these days? You aren't going to believe this, but I got an amazing call today."

"We aren't interested in selling, if that's what you got on your mind." The smile was suddenly gone from Mr. Burdett's face, and he looked grim. "We already said no."

Willow watched the couple, seeing the look that flashed between them, then disappeared. She thought it was fear. But then, the determined, grim look was back on his face.

"Somebody already approached you on this? A gigantic offer for the farm?"

"Some guy was here yesterday, trying to convince us to sell. Wouldn't take no for an answer. Practically had to throw him off the place."

"Was his name Charley Morse?"

"Didn't get so far as to ask the man's name. Didn't want

to know it. He was a pushy, rude guy, flashing papers in my face, and trying to intimidate the missus. I didn't like him a bit. Not a bit.''

Willow thought back to her conversation with the rude, abrupt man. She remembered the flash of concern she had felt, the feeling that something wasn't quite right.

''Has he been back? Have you heard from him again?''

''Not a word, until you arrived. Willow, what is going on that you would get involved with a mean man like that?''

''I haven't met him. He called the office. Offered this outrageous price. I thought you deserved to know. You know, in case you needed the money.''

''I'll never need money enough to deal with a slimy guy like that. I love my farm, even though I can't take very good care of it. But we got two cows, and two horses, and some chickens, and I can take care of them just fine. We got what we need, right on this place. There's some things that are more important than money, you know.''

Willow smiled fondly. ''How well I know. You're a wise man. Listen, he'll be calling me, I'm sure, to find out if I approached you. I'll tell him to get lost, maybe even find him another place, to keep him off your backs. If you hear from him again, just call, okay?''

She left a card on the table, listing her office phone, her home phone, and her mobile phone. Mrs. Burdett loaded her up with a basket of muffins to share with Maggie and the kids at the farm.

''Tell her I'm making apple pies with the last of the apples from last year.'' She motioned to two bushels of apples that sat on the kitchen counter. ''I'll send over a few when they're done.''

With a wave and a promise to keep in touch, Willow left the farm, trying to calm the nagging feeling of apprehension that had taken hold of her.

She was anxiously awaiting the phone call from Charley Morse the next morning, when the temporary office assistant arrived. Her name was Gail, and she seemed bright and enthusiastic. Willow showed her around the office, and then introduced her to Mildred, who was planning to brief her on her duties.

Gail had just taken over the phones when the call arrived. "Excuse me, sir, this is not Willow, this is Gail." The woman's face turned red. "If you'll be patient for a moment, I'll transfer you to her desk." She pushed the hold button.

"Willow, it's a guy named Charley. Man, is he rude!"

Willow sighed. "You bet he is. Transfer him over here. Heaven knows we need clients, but this one we can do without."

Her phone buzzed, and she picked it up.

"Willow Blake. How can I help you?"

"Cut to the the chase, Willow. Tell me about the Burdetts. Do we have a deal?"

"Of course you don't have a deal. You send me out there looking like a fool when you already knew they weren't interested in selling."

"Your job is to sell, babe. Can't you convince them to listen?"

"No deal, Mr. Morse. The Burdetts want to stay right where they are, so the case is closed. How about looking at another piece of property? There are several small farms for sale—"

The man on the other end of the phone exploded. "I want to buy that farm, babe. What's it going to take?"

"It's going to take another lifetime, Mr. Morse, because they aren't going to sell. And you're going to need another lifetime, Mr. Morse, if you call me babe one more time in that demeaning tone of voice."

"You broads are all alike. Can't take the heat."

"Good-bye, Mr. Morse. . . . I'm going to hang up now."

"You're a no-good incompetent—"

Willow slowly hung up the phone, taking a deep breath, and trying to force the man's words out of her head. *Detach. It can't get to you if you don't let it.* She let the anger flow through her body, trying to keep memories at bay.

Name-calling. Blaming. She had grown up with it, letting each verbal blow take a chip off her soul. But no more. She knew who she was today, and she didn't have to let the words hurt.

"Wow," commented Gail, when the conversation ended. "You handled that pretty well. I hope all your clients aren't like that. A guy like that can really ruin your day."

Willow smiled. "He's one of a kind, thank goodness. But I don't think he'll call again." He might bother the Burdetts, though, she realized. He hadn't given up on the thought of getting the farm. She'd plan to stop by to check in with them.

The rest of the day passed quickly with Willow answering real estate questions on the phone, showing town houses to a newly married couple, writing ad copy for the newspaper.

When the workday was over, Willow changed into a pair of shorts and a T-shirt before leaving the office. The group at the AIDS home was working on a project, building a wheelchair ramp by the side door, and she had offered to help. She had also contributed the money for the lumber and materials to do the job.

The bank may have let them down, but she was determined to get the job done. She climbed into her car and drove across town, letting the warm summer air rush though her short blond hair. Country music blared from the radio, and she sang along.

She'd spend a few hours holding boards, measuring, sawing, and hammering. There was a warm sense of camaraderie as they worked together on the ramp. Two neighbors joined them when they came home from work and saw the work in progress. Willow felt good. The neighborhood had finally accepted their newest residents, respecting them, and even offering a helping hand.

They were almost finished with the job, collecting scraps and organizing tools, when an ancient Volkswagen pulled up. A tiny woman emerged, dressed in gray. Willow recognized the spunky nun from the bank meeting.

"Hi, Sister!" they called. "Come to hammer?"

"I wouldn't know what to do with a hammer if I had to." She laughed. "I brought food." She reached into the backseat of the VW and pulled out a stack of pizza boxes. "I'm glad you got some building supplies."

"Thanks to Willow," one man said softly. "She contributed the materials."

Willow saw the nun watching her intently. "I didn't think Willow was going to let the bank win on this one."

Willow smiled, embarrassed with the praise. "This is just the start. "I'm going to start a fund."

"And I'm going to do a little arm twisting and help. We'll get some contributions and pledges. You're not alone on this one, Willow!"

"Thanks." Her eyes felt suspiciously moist, but she had no intention of crying. She shook her head, and grabbed for another piece of pizza. "I love pizza. The perfect food." Everybody laughed, and the tension left her.

Exhausted after working at the barn, she went home to bed, falling asleep instantly. She was so tired that she totally forgot her plan to phone the Burdetts to report her problems with the charming Charley Morse.

Chapter Six

The next morning was a beautiful one. The June sun was bright and the sky was a terrific shade of blue. Willow loved the summer smells as she drove down the country roads on her way to town. The scent of honeysuckle, which grew abundantly along the road, mingled with the pungent smell of rich tilled soil and sprouting green fields. She never got tired of the beauty around her.

She was wearing green today, a trim, stylish suit with a boxy jacket that almost matched the length of her short skirt. A lacy white camisole peeked out from under the jacket. Her green heels were of medium height—low enough to still be comfortable, but high enough to proclaim her comfort with her height. She was striking.

It was almost 9:00 A.M. when she parked her Miata in front of Reynolds Realty. Gail was alone in the office, taking phone calls and writing messages with a sense of ease. She pushed a pile of messages toward Willow as she arrived, nodding her head in acknowledgment, but not breaking the conversation she was having on the phone.

Willow was impressed with the style and competence of the temporary receptionist, and took her pile of messages with a grateful sigh. Plopping down at her desk, she sorted through the stack.

The appraisal on Manxo's future estate was finished; papers would now be drawn for the final closing. A family she had been working with had driven past a house they would like to see, whenever Willow could schedule an appointment with the owner. The Sunday ad copy was due at the local newpaper by the 5:00 P.M. deadline.

All were normal and expected messages until the last. Mrs. Burdett, the memo said, had called at 8:02, right when the office had opened. She had asked for Willow, and then the call had been abruptly cut off. She hadn't called back.

Willow turned to Gail, who had just hung up the phone. "This call from Mrs. Burdett . . . there was no message at all?"

"Actually, it was kind of strange. I guess she's elderly . . . her voice sounded very soft and tired. But she got no farther than asking for you—then the connection was broken. I'm sorry." Gail was watching the worried expression on Willow's face. Calls could be disrupted for many reasons, but Willow looked concerned.

"You don't have to apologize, Gail. It's obvious you're doing a great job. I'm just worried about the lady. I think I'll drive over to her place and see what's on her mind. I'll be back."

At that moment, the door of the office opened, and a uniformed deliveryman entered with a large overnight mailing envelope. "W. Blake? Would you sign for this?" Willow rose to greet him, taking the envelope and signing the form.

When he had left, she opened the package, pulling out the contents curiously. Papers. Real estate papers. She unfolded the completed agreement of sale and read it carefully. She sucked in her breath.

The Burdetts' name leaped off the page at her. The form was duly signed and witnessed. The Burdetts' had sold their ten-acre farm to Charles Morse for the sum of $500,000 dollars, payment in cash. A certified copy of the title search, receipt for the money, and all of the necessary papers for the property transfer were enclosed.

Willow was stunned. She riffled through the papers, which all appeared to be in order. The deal, though totally unorthodox, seemed legal. A note addressed to her was enclosed.

Please file the necessary paperwork to transfer this property, submitting a bill for your commission and any incurred costs to Mr. Porter Blank, at the law firm of William Harrison and Associates, Ryerstown, who holds the power of attorney to conduct any business necessary for this transaction. Thank you very much.
													Charles Morse

The note was typed; the signature was scrawled. In it's correctness and politeness, the note didn't resemble Charley Morse at all. She looked at the agreement again. Charley had signed the bottom, as had his witness, none other than Mr. Porter Blank himself.

For a moment, she tried to feel enthusiastic. There would be a big commission, for practically no work at all. A salesperson's dream had just landed in her lap. But her mind would not let her think in those terms. There was something wrong here. She had seen the Burdetts only the day before, and they had adamantly refused to even *think* about parting with their property. Even if they had changed their minds, it wouldn't have happened so quickly . . . so absolutely. It just didn't ring true.

A thousand scenarios started building in her mind— threats and coercion forcing the little couple to sell . . . greedy developers putting undue pressure on defenseless farmers. Her imagination sometimes tended to be a little wild. But still . . .

The law firm listed as the attorney for the sale was located right across the street from her office. It took less than a split second to decide what to do. She would simply stop over and ask the attorney in question about the sale. He had signed the form, he had been present, the papers were in order.

A short conversation could relieve her anxieties about the deal, and then a quick trip to the farm to congratulate the Burdetts on the sale would assuage any worries she had about their sudden change of mind. They had been offered a mound of money, enough to entice even the staunchest landowner to reevaluate their stand. So she'd check it out, and then get to work.

It was only a few short steps to the law office across the street. She bounded up the stately porch steps with her usual energy, coming to the front door which bore an elegant brass-plated message. PLEASE ENTER.

The solid wood door swung open effortlessly, making no sound as she stepped into the elegant foyer that doubled as a reception area. A regal-looking older woman sat at the desk, her hair neatly pulled into a chignon, her beige wool suit reflecting efficiency and good taste.

"May I help you?"

"I'm Willow Blake, from Reynolds Realty across the street. May I speak with Porter Blank?"

The receptionist smiled without emotion, the kind of smile that is like a pleasant mask, hiding the thoughts behind its wearer's eyes.

"And you have an appointment?" She looked down, scanning her book.

"Well, no. I received papers from him, and I had a few questions. . . ."

"I see. Perhaps we could make you an appointment."

"To be honest with you, ma'am, I don't want to wait to make an appointment. This is important, and I need to see him immediately."

"I'm terribly sorry, Ms. Blake, but you'll need to make

an appointment." She glanced at the book. "Perhaps the day after tomorrow at 2:00 P.M.?"

"Won't you just ask him? If he has just a minute."

"I will not."

"Please, it's so important."

"We have a procedure here, Ms. Blake. I have a job to do. That job entails keeping order in this office. I can put you down for the day after tomorrow at 2:00 P.M."

Like a volcano getting ready to erupt, Willow felt her frustration building to explode. She had a terrible feeling of urgency about the deal. But she didn't have a choice at the moment. The dragon lady wasn't going to let her talk to the popular Mr. Porter Blank. She'd have to go to the Burdetts' instead.

Rockford Harrison had been sitting in his office, at the usual place, looking out the window, as had become one of his favorite pastimes. He had seen the golden girl emerge from the realty office, and had watched in awe as she had crossed the street in those long, appealing strides, marching right up to his very office building.

She had been in his dreams, and now she was in his foyer. But as seemed to be usual, things were not going well. He had heard the exchange between the blond and the rather forceful receptionist his uncle had employed to protect the firm members from unexpected clients. But he had heard the need in Willow's voice, and the exasperation she felt. He felt drawn to her.

Willow Blake, she had introduced herself. Reynolds Realty. He knew the identity of the golden girl. Without thinking about decorum, or propriety, for once in his life, Rockford jumped at the chance to meet the woman who intrigued him.

Giving up on the receptionist, Willow had taken a deep breath, spun on her heel, and walked to the door. As her hand touched the knob, a low, chuckling voice could be heard behind her.

"Ah, Ms. Blake. Perhaps I could be of some assistance in this matter."

She turned and looked into the deepest, darkest eyes she had ever seen, and almost instantly, felt her usually stable knees go weak. She opened her mouth, then closed it again. For some reason, all of her body parts seemed to be having difficulty in doing their job.

"Porter Blank?" she said finally, almost in a whisper, eyes locked with his.

"Not a chance. Harrison. Rockford Harrison. But perhaps I can help. Why don't you come this way into my office."

"But Mr. Harrison—" began the dragon lady in a slighted, offended voice. "She has no appointment."

Rockford Harrison put back his head and laughed then, instantly noticing the way that Willow's eyes lit up at the sound of his voice. Her eyes were doing something to him, deep down inside. He felt like he was a little short of oxygen, and it made him feel almost giddy.

"It's okay, Prudence," he gentled the ruffled receptionist. "She has no appointment, but then again, I have practically no clients. So I don't mind giving the time." He smiled at the older lady, and she was instantly placated.

"Well, if it's no hardship, Mr. Harrison."

"None at all. We must go out of our way to keep our clients happy." He took the astonished Willow by the arm and led her gently around the corner to his office, leaving a puzzled receptionist behind.

"She doesn't know how easy she got off," he said with a conspiratorial wink at Willow. "I know a librarian who's probably still trying to refile the books at the return desk from his encounter with you."

Willow blushed, then giggled. "You were there? I get a little carried away."

"It was inspirational. Several people who were in line did the same thing. The return pile overtook the desk. I doubt that that man will ever be rude to a customer again."

Willow laughed.

"Now, again. I'm Rockford Harrison, another attorney for the firm. What can I help you with?"

He stuck out his hand to shake hers, his large fingers curling around hers naturally, the warmth of his skin making her tingle. "Uh, I'm Willow Blake. From Reynolds Realty across the street. I received a surprise package of real estate papers from Mr. Porter this morning, and I have a lot of questions about the deal. I was hoping he could ease my mind."

"He's not here."

"Will he be in later? When do you think I could talk to him?"

"Evidently, he called in last night and said he was taking a few days off. We don't expect him until the day after tomorrow, from what I understand."

A wave of apprehension rushed over her, and it showed in her face.

"Willow, what's the problem? This looks serious."

"I have no idea if it's serious or not. It's just strange. And I get this funny feeling that things are just not right."

"Sit. Tell me." He watched her fold her long legs and sit in one of the Queen Anne chairs that were placed around the room. She looked so good there, so natural.

She eyed him carefully, amazed at the trust she felt for the handsome stranger. She told him the story about Charley Morse and the Burdetts. He listened attentively.

"So maybe it's worth a ride out to the farm. Maybe hearing the Burdetts' explanation will make the thing clear. Or else . . ."

"Or else I'll know that there's something wrong with the deal."

He nodded wordlessly.

"Thanks," she said, standing to go. "Thanks for listening. Even if you don't have answers, it reaffirmed what I was thinking. I'll go out there now and see them."

"Care for company?"

She stopped dead in her tracks, meeting the magical eyes again. "You'd come?"

"In a New York minute. Things are rather . . . slow around here." He gestured around the spacious office. "This is the most excitement I've seen in a while."

She grinned at him, and his stomach immediately tightened. He was amazed at the effect she had on him. He wondered if she could tell.

"Well, let's go, counselor. I'm driving. Of course, you're on your own clearing things with Prudence out there."

"I'm not afraid of Prudence. I'll just threaten to leave you here to reshuffle her Rolodex file. That'll keep her in line."

"Boy, you play hardball."

They escaped out the front door, ignoring the disapproving glance that Prudence offered. Practically running to the Miata sitting down the block, they were laughing by the time Willow pulled into the Main Street traffic.

Feeling like an errant child who had escaped from school, Rockford looked over at the amazing woman who held the wheel. The wind was softly ruffling her short blond hair; her face was flushed and alive as she sang along to the radio. There was no pretense, no self-consciousness. She was just Willow, and she was beautiful. With a deep breath, he pulled his eyes away, watching the roadway, anxiously realizing that he was sorely in danger of losing his heart.

Chapter Seven

Silence was the first thing that Rockford noticed as they pulled the small car into the rutted driveway of the Burdett farm. He wasn't used to solitude. Growing up on his family's extensive estate north of New York, and then working in the bustling world of the city, he had never experienced the quiet that crept around them now.

The car bounced along, making him grab onto the dashboard once or twice. They came to a stop near the front door of the farmhouse.

"Boy, it's lonely out here. I don't see anybody." Rockford looked around, noticing the rocking chairs on the porch, the painted butter churn standing in the flower garden. "But it's nice."

"The pickup truck is gone. Maybe they've gone out."

They walked together up the worn porch steps, and Willow knocked on the door. As on her last trip, the wooden door stood open, and the screen door was closed.

"Mrs. Burdett? Mr. Burdett? Are you here? It's Willow Blake." She peered in through the screen, listening for any kitchen sounds that might be heard. But all they heard was silence.

"Something's wrong. I can feel it. They're not here. The door's wide open, the truck's gone. . . ." She could hear the anxiety in her own voice.

"Don't get worried, Willow. Probably she's in the bathroom, or upstairs." He raised his hand, and pounded hard

48

on the door frame. "Hello? Hello?" The deep timbre of his voice echoed through the house. No one answered. If they were home, they would have heard it.

With a quick movement, Willow scooted past him, pushing open the screen door, and slipping down the hall to the kitchen.

"Willow, come back here. You can't go prancing into people's houses. It's against the law." His feet started following her, against his better judgment.

Willow's voice was grim. "Maybe for you, Harrison, but not for me. Something's wrong here, and I'm really worried. I want to look around."

"Can you imagine what these poor people will say if they pull in here, and you're slinking around their house? You don't have any cause for this. You're letting your imagination get the best of you."

"At least I have an imagination." She was in the kitchen now. It was stone silent, with sunny rays coming in the back window and making a pattern on the linoleum floor. "I also have a signed agreement of sale for this property, listing me as the realtor of record. I think the deal stinks, but meanwhile, I have an obligation to look out for the people I represent."

His eyes narrowed, as he watched her move around. He followed her, having no idea what she was up to. She paused by the kitchen sink, where an empty bushel basket sat on the counter. She opened the fridge, which held only a few supplies. She looked in the oven and found it empty and cold.

"There are no pies. Something's going on."

Rockford looked at her as if she had rocks in her head. She turned and looked straight into his eyes, and he could see the emotion there. Something inside of him contracted, and he had to fight the urge to put an arm around her.

He was practical, instead. "I don't know what you're talking about."

"The pies. She was going to make pies yesterday. Said she'd bring us some. The apples are gone, but there's no pies. Somebody took the pies."

Was he dealing with a fruitcake?

"Willow, maybe they are delivering the pies right now, did you think of that?"

Her eyes flashed relief for a minutes, wanting to accept his explanation. But then she started darting around the kitchen, looking in the cabinets under the sink. She pulled out an empty trash can, staring at it for a minute.

"Find the trash. Go out and find the trash cans. I have to go around back and look for something."

He followed her out the door, feeling like he had stepped into some fantasy. A gorgeous blond had instructed him to find the trash cans, and he was going to obey. He had no idea why, and he didn't much care. But he found the cans. They were right by the back door.

"Trash cans, Willow." She had moved away from the house, toward the barn, but she came running back. He pulled the lid off the metal container. The smell of apples rose to greet them.

"Just apple cores and peelings."

"I knew it. I could just feel it. Call the police."

He blew out his breath slowly. "One more time. I'm sure this is significant, and it's some gigantic flaw in my reasoning that I'm not following you, but humor me. Why are we calling the police about the apple cores?"

"Because the Burdetts didn't put them there. Something's happened to them, and it must have happened last night when she was making pies. Farmers like the Burdetts don't throw out apple remnants, Rockford. They'd either feed them to the animals, or bury them in the compost pile. Somebody else did that. Somebody cleaned up, and tried to make it look like things were all right . . . but they're not." She started walking determinedly toward the barn.

"Dare I ask . . ." He had to walk quickly to keep up with her long strides. He shuddered as he watched the dust flurry around his black wing tips as he stepped quickly to her side.

"I've got to check the animals. The Burdetts love their critters."

The barn door creaked loudly as she pulled it open, and slipped inside into its cool darkness. The pungent smell of animal mixed with the sweet odor of hay filled his nostrils. Believe it or not, Rockford Harrison was in a barn.

Instantly, Willow was all over the place. She removed the long green jacket of her suit, and hung it on a wooden peg by the door. Talking lowly and smoothly, she approached the two horses that stood silently in their stalls. He followed her, mesmerized, and watched her nonstop action.

"Attaboy, good boy," she cooed, as she filled a food bucket with some kind of grain and then ran a long hose to the stalls and filled the two water troughs. The horses watched her with mournful eyes, seeming to accept her ministrations. The horses didn't exactly look like the specimens in the movies, gallant and energetic and charging with the cavalry on their backs. These looked more like candidates for the glue factory. Advanced age, and graying noses. But what did he know? This was the closest he had ever been to a horse in his life. He kept his thoughts to himself.

He followed her to a shed attached to the side of the barn, where she flung a few handfuls of grain to the chickens who began squawking as soon as they came into sight.

"I can't believe this. This is awful. We've got to find these people. These animals need care."

She headed back into the barn with Rockford still trotting

after her. "Are we done here? Should we go back into town?"

That was wishful thinking on his part. "We've got to take care of the cows. They're already going to be in bad shape."

Take care of the cows? "Cows? Do we need to feed them?"

"First we have to milk them." She had grabbed two aluminum buckets from the wall, and had tucked two stools under her arm. She headed to the back of the barn, and pushed open the back door. Sunlight poured in, illuminating the stalls they had not visited yet. Two giant black-and-white creatures came into view. Cows. She scurried around them, and he heard her swear gently at what she found.

She turned toward him, holding out a bucket, not saying a word. He stared at her.

"You have to be kidding. Tell me you're kidding."

"These cows missed their early morning milking, and they're in bad shape. We don't have time to find somebody else to do the job . . . it just needs to be done."

He still stared at her blankly.

"Uh, my suit. This is an Italian import. Pure silk. My shirt is custom-made. I'm already wondering if I'll ever get the smell of this barn out of my clothes."

He saw the disappointment in her eyes, and his jaw tensed.

"Really, Willow, I'm not a farmer. I'm an attorney. I don't do cows. Let's go and find somebody who can take care of these cows."

"I already found somebody who can take care of these cows. Me. If you don't want to help, that's okay. But I'm going to get the job done. I just thought it would cut down on the time."

Her eyes were blazing, and they were a most remarkable color, even in the dimness of the barn. They met his with an intensity that rocked him to his bones, and he felt his heart begin to hammer.

"You're not worried about your clothes?" He gestured to the lacy camisole she wore over her suit skirt.

She smiled then, raising a hand that was smudged with barn dirt from carrying the stools. With deliberation, she wiped her hand on the side of her skirt, leaving a trail of dirt behind.

"I never worry about my clothes, counselor," she said softly, those hypnotic eyes meeting his again. "Clothes are only props. But life is a priority. I only worry about helpless people, and helpless animals, and I help whenever I can. And right now I'm worried about Mr. Burdett's cows. It's the principle of the thing. So excuse me while I milk."

She squatted on a stool by the farthest cow, and within seconds, he could hear her gentle cooing, and hear the rhythmic sound of the milk splashing into the bucket.

He sighed just once, filling his lungs with air that reeked of barn, and peeled off his coat. Cuff links clinked into his pants pocket, and shirtsleeves were soon rolled up to his elbows. He said a prayer for his wing tips, and then stepped to the bucket and stool that stood next to the second cow.

"Okay, Willow, talk me through this thing."

So she did. He listened; he followed directions. He milked the cow. It really wasn't so bad, he realized, once you got the hang of it. He could almost feel the relief of the cow as the bucket filled and the strain left her udders. "It's okay, girl," he said gently, and was rewarded by a soft moo. He couldn't believe how happy he felt.

His back was stiff by the time he was finished, from sitting tensely hunched over on the little stool. His suit, he figured, was going to be a casualty—his aim hadn't been too perfect when he'd first begun. But his shirt would clean up, and probably his shoes, too, for that matter. But Willow had been absolutely right—it wasn't important.

With bucket in hand, he turned and faced her. Her face was dirty, but smiling, and he felt a wave of emotion as he looked at her.

"It's the principle of the thing," she had said. Just like Peter. He had scoffed at Peter so many times, instead of taking his example. But today he had listened to Willow, and he had learned a lot. Peter would like that.

"We probably should dump the milk. The buckets weren't sterilized, and we don't want to risk making more problems. But we kept the cows healthy, and that's what counts." She put things away, and began closing up the barn. "I'll have Maggie contact someone if we can't find the Burdetts."

They walked silently to the car, holding their jackets. She turned suddenly to him, and he almost ran into her. They were standing face-to-face, just inches apart. "You did a great job in there, Rockford. I know that's not your thing, but you got the job done. Thanks." She leaned up then, just slightly because she was so tall, and placed a soft, quick kiss on his surprised lips.

Then she opened the car door and quickly hopped inside, leaving him next to the car. Stunned, he stepped around the car, and got into the passenger seat. He wanted more than a kiss. He was absolutely astonished with himself.

The car bounced back down the lane to the road, and he watched her profile as she concentrated on the road before her. She was magnificent, breathtaking. He wished he knew what she was thinking.

The truth was, Willow was thinking many things. She was thinking about the Burdetts, and how she was going to get the police to pay attention to their sudden disappearance. She was thinking about the animals, and how she was going to have them taken care of in their owners' absence.

But mostly, she was thinking of the tall, dark, handsome

lawyer who was sitting in the car next to her. There was something about him that set her on fire, and she was more than uncomfortable about it. She had kissed him almost to spite herself, to prove to herself that it didn't matter. But it did. It mattered. He mattered. And it was causing feelings in her that were new and unsettling.

In the barn, she had heard him gently reassuring the cow, his voice low and soft. She had seen his caring actions and touch, and her mind had begun working overtime, creating fantasies that were wreaking havoc with her self-control. And now she had gone and kissed him.

She had the grace to blush as she drove the rest of the way into town.

Chapter Eight

After dropping Rockford off in town, Willow drove back to her cottage on the farm to shower and change her clothes. Despite her defiant gesture to prove a point to "Righteous Rockford," as she had already dubbed him, she didn't enjoy having barn dirt on her work clothes.

She got cleaned up quickly, deciding to cancel or rearrange her real estate plans for the rest of the day. She pulled on jeans, boots, and a sweatshirt and headed out for the barn to find Maggie.

She found her practically upside down, her head and arms hidden as she bent over to investigate the inside of a large feed barrel.

"Is this an ostrich imitation, Mag?" She laughed, peering into the barrel at her friend.

"There it is!" the older woman exclaimed, stretching back out of the barrel and standing up straight. "There's a tiny mouse hole way down by the bottom. I couldn't locate it from the outside. But from the inside, I saw the daylight come through. I've got to patch it to keep the critters away from the feed."

"What a detective. You sound like Columbo."

"Just get me a raincoat. . . . Now what brings you around here in the middle of the day? Run out of houses to sell?"

Willow explained the problem with the Burdetts. Maggie's brow was creased as she listened.

"Doesn't sound like the Burdetts, going off and all, selling quick like that. I have a feeling you're right. Something's going on. Have you gone to the police?''

"I'm on my way. But they're going to tell me it's too early to consider them missing persons . . . they don't care much about milking schedules, according to this city-type attorney I talked to. Supposedly you have to wait two days."

"Tell that to the cows. Listen, I'll take the trailer over and pick up the livestock if they're not back by dinnertime. We can take care of things here. And I'll leave a note so if they had an emergency, and then came home, they'll know where everybody is. I think they'd approve of that."

Willow's face showed how grateful she was. "I'm going to try to find them. They couldn't have just disappeared."

Maggie nodded. "Just take that city-slicker lawman with you, Willow, to keep you safe."

The thought made Maggie laugh. She pictured the Italian silk suit, and the fancy leather shoes. "I'm not exactly sure how much of a Columbo he would be—he looks a bit . . . stiff."

Maggie looked back at her with wise eyes. "He milked a cow, right? He got the job done. Can't ask for more than that. People can't help what they are, what they come from. It's what they *do* that counts. Didn't anybody ever tell you not to judge a book by its cover? People can surprise you, really surprise you, if you give them a chance."

Willow looked thoughtful.

"Call me," Maggie added as she headed out the door, "if you don't want me to pick up the stock at the Burdetts. If I don't hear from you, I'm heading over at 5:00 P.M., so I can be back for the evening lessons. The blind kids can learn how to milk a cow. Now *that* should be a challenge."

The mental picture made Willow smile. Maggie would do it, too, proving once again to handicapped kids that they could rise above their limitations.

She sped out the door to face her own challenges.

* * *

The police were overworked and not overly excited about her request. Probably more because they wanted to be polite, a patient officer took down the information that Willow provided.

"In a couple of days we'll look into it if they don't show up. Missing apple pies are simply not evidence of foul play." He was distant but courteous, reciting the rules.

Willow grimaced at his words. She was disappointed, but glad she had made the report. It was going to be up to her, if she didn't want to wait for police help. She drove back up to the farm, and spent several hours searching for anything that might lead to the Burdetts. She was tired and frustrated by the time Maggie's truck and trailer lumbered up the drive.

She helped load the large animals onto the truck, then together they captured the chickens and put them in wire carrying cases. Maggie posted a note to the Burdetts, tacking it to a prominent post in the barn where it couldn't be missed.

Willow followed the truck back to the farm, settled the animals, and then joined Maggie in the lesson for the blind. The first several minutes were spent explaining the intricacies of milking, followed by a hilarious but wholehearted attempt by the children to milk the cows.

When they were done, they had two contented cows, several proud children, and a very wet Willow. Once more she returned to the cottage to shower and change.

She was tired when she crawled into her bed that night, still worried about the Burdetts, but knowing that their beloved stock was well settled in the back of Maggie's barn.

Her sleep was broken and unsettled, with recurrent dreams about a tall dark lawyer whose eyes reached right into her soul, and whose touch made her wild with longing.

* * *

After his coerced lesson in cow milking, Rockford had returned home to the apartment he shared with George. The clothes, he decided, were casualties of the day, but expendable. He smiled as he climbed into a clean sweat suit and laced up his sneakers. He had milked a cow. Incredible. Peter would have been proud.

He thought about Peter a lot these days, probably more than he ever had. But instead of just focusing on Peter's death, he had begun to focus on Peter's life. "The principle of the thing," as his buddy had often said. He saved the cow, and ruined his suit. He shoved the rumpled ball of imported silk into the kitchen trash can, just as George came bounding in the door.

"What's that?" she said, quickly grabbing the wrinkled suit from the can. "Throwing it away? We'll recycle it." She stuffed it into a yellow shopping bag in the corner of the kitchen, suddenly sniffing the air. "It smells kind of . . . farmy in here."

So he told her the story, and got it over with. He knew she'd laugh, and he was proven right. She giggled, she chortled, she guffawed. He wanted to strangle her, but he kept up his narrative until the end. It was harder than any jury he had ever addressed.

George had recognized the flamboyant Willow from her brother's description, but she followed a flash of instinct and didn't let on that she knew her as she listened to his tale.

Aside from the comical moments of imagining her staid brother with his head in a trash can, investigating apple peels, and perching on a rickety milking stool filling a dented bucket with determination, George seemed to pick up on Willow's concern for the Burdetts right away.

"So the animals will be cared for? And the police will be notified of the couple's absence? I must say I agree with your young friend that something out of the usual has occurred here.''

''Why do you women jump to these conclusions? The real estate papers all looked in order. I can't help but wonder if the couple just decided to sell the farm, stock and all, and took off for a new life. It's a lot of money, you know. But Willow says the same as you. She's making arrangements for the animals, and she said she'd report things to the police.''

''And I'm sure she will. She sounds like the kind of person who gets things done.''

George smiled brightly then, seemingly changing the subject.

''I have a project for you. I need your help. We're establishing a fund for resources for the local AIDS home. It's a way that you can get involved in the community, Rockford, with all those big bucks of yours. Will you help fund it?''

Rockford laughed. ''You're always up to some crazy project or another, Georgina. If I remember correctly, you gave a startling portion of your inheritance to build a hospital on an Indian reservation in New Mexico several years ago.''

''It's a wonderful facility. Efficient and full of heart.''

''Then there was the estate you purchased for abused women. . . .''

''Still going strong. But that was Peter's idea, really.''

Rockford froze. ''Peter?''

''Of course. It was his way of coming to grips with his past. You remember his lovely mom, who struggled so hard to bring him up on her own? He remembered the early days when his father had been around, taking out his frustrations on his family. He wanted to help other people who had to go through something like that. So I helped him. Didn't you know?''

"No . . . I didn't."

"Too busy off making money, and wining and dining in those posh New York clubs, I suppose. Maybe he thought you'd laugh at him. He didn't have money, but he had brains and he had heart. He set things up, and I helped with the funds. He wanted to make a difference. So he did."

It was simple, really, if you thought of it. Rockford felt the guilt rumbling in him, building like an intense inferno. People like Peter and George spent their time and their fortunes caring about others, and he spent his . . . on himself.

"Feeling guilty?" George's tinkling laugh was full of love and felt like welcomed water on a raging fire. "It's just that I need you, Rockford. I've exhausted my own resources, and Peter . . . well, his memory will live on, but his energy is greatly missed. What do you say?"

"As usual, my petite but powerful sibling, your arrow has found its mark. You have a way of making me look full tilt into the mirror, not unlike the kind of self-appraisal that Peter demanded. You make me feel like a heel, then you applaud me for my potential." He marched across the room and picked up his tiny sister, holding her in the air.

"Your nagging little ways are making progress, Georgina. I will stop at the bank tomorrow and give money to your trust. Fifty thousand dollars will be a small price to pay to get you off my back."

He kissed her on the top of the head, and then lowered her to the ground. "I've been surrounded by bossing, demanding females all day, it seems. First there's Prudence in the office, then the world-conquering Willow, and last but certainly not least, an aggravating angel named Georgina who picks things out of the trash, and tells me things about my best friend that even I didn't know. I'm going for a good jog to forget the lot of you." He laughed.

Christine Bush

"Good. Get in shape. We need you to have plenty of strength to fight all the battles we have lined up for you."

He got serious for a minute, looking like a black cloud had passed over him. "I'm not good at fighting battles, George. I've never been committed to anything except making money. You know that. Don't expect more of me than I am."

"Don't worry, brother," George said to the door after he had left for his run, "I know exactly what you are, even if you don't know. You'll find yourself yet, Rockford Farquahar Harrison III, if I have anything to say about it!"

Maybe with Willow's help too, she thought with a smile. After all, anyone who could cajole the big bad lawyer to milk a cow had many talents and abilities! George felt happy and optimistic as she planned the next activities of her day.

Chapter Nine

Patience was a virtue that Willow knew she didn't possess. It was the hardest thing in the world for her to wait . . . so the next day dragged on endlessly. It was raining and dreary, and the real estate office was quiet. Gail busily and cheerfully typed at her desk, and Willow spent the time updating files and writing ad copy for her listings.

She was biding time until the elusive Mr. Blank returned to his law office. She had even called the ever-delightful Prudence and had scheduled an official appointment with the man for tomorrow when he returned. She hoped that he could shed some light on what had gone on with the Burdetts. Early in the morning, she had returned to the farm, but had seen no sign that anyone had even been there since she and Maggie had rescued the animals.

Charley Morse had wanted a quick and immediate sale, but there was no sign of activity to indicate why. Possessed with a good dose of curiosity and an imagination that was so well developed that it often got her into trouble, she still couldn't come up with a scenario to explain what had happened. So she waited. Impatiently. Because she couldn't think of a single other thing to do until she talked to Porter Blank.

Taking a break from her paperwork, she was in the process of making coffee when the phone rang.

"Willow," whispered Gail, who had picked up the phone, "it's for you. It's the police."

Willow darted back to her desk.

"This is Willow Blake. How can I help you?"

"Good afternoon, Ms. Blake. This is Detective Dunn from the police. We spoke yesterday concerning the Burdetts."

Willow's heart was hammering. "Yes? Did you find them? Did something happen?"

"We haven't found them, I'm sorry to say. But we are taking your concern seriously at this point. Their empty truck was found early this morning. It had evidently crashed and was stuck in a ditch, about twenty miles from town. The tow truck is bringing it in."

"Oh, no, was there any sign of them?"

"None at all. The truck was empty except for some trash. We are pretty sure it was stolen, so we're going to dust it for prints and evidence samples. I thought you ought to know. We're pursuing the couple's disappearance."

"You should have listened to me yesterday," she complained, her worry showing in her voice. "Those two poor old people have been in trouble for over twenty-four hours. We have to find them."

"I was just following missing persons regulations, Ms. Blake. And now I'm doing everything I can. I'm calling to ask you to bring down the real estate papers that were delivered to you. We're going to run an investigation on this Charles Morse."

Willow rummaged in her desk for the brown envelope. "Great. I'm on my way."

With a few words of instruction to Gail, she gathered up her things, and lunged out the door.

At least, she attempted to lunge out the door. She collided with a large, moving obstacle who was attempting to walk into the office. Broad shoulders and strong arms caught her before she went off balance.

"Whoa, Willow," a deep voice said. "Were you shot

out of a cannon? Slow down before you take out an innocent bystander.''

She raised her head and looked into the dark eyes that had mesmerized her before. ''Rockford. I don't think the word innocent applies here.''

He laughed, reluctantly letting her go. ''Where's the fire?''

''No fire. Truck crash.'' She filled him in on the details from the police station.

''Let's go,'' he said, swiveling on his heel, and heading back out the door, with one arm protectively on her elbow.

It felt good. It felt bad. She had been so happy to see him, so happy to see his intelligent face recording her words, and caring about what was going on. She had felt a strong sense of camaraderie and partnership. She had felt like she was not alone. But then her mind had kicked in, alerting her to the dangers of depending on someone, the foolishness of trusting, and then getting hurt. Her father's angry face flashed across her mind, leaving pain in its stead.

She pulled her arm away. Rockford was puzzled by her action, but he tried not to let the hurt show.

''How about if I drive?'' he said instead. ''My car is right across the street.''

''That's okay,'' she said automatically, opening the door of the Miata and climbing in before he had a chance to object. ''I'd rather drive.''

He shrugged and folded his body into the little car, while she started the engine and pulled out into the road. Her hands were clenched on the steering wheel, exerting control on the Miata, which had its top up in deference to the rain. *I'm not dependent,* her mind chanted. *I don't need anybody or anything. I'm in charge of my own life.* Slowly, the visions and memories of her father receded.

''Kind of touchy, aren't you, Willow?'' She looked over toward him and his eyes looked wise.

She smiled. "Maybe a bit. Old conditioning. I like to be in control, I guess."

"That's okay. You can trust me, Willow. I won't try to take control."

"Trust isn't my strong point, counselor."

"You have to be careful who you trust, that's for sure. But trust isn't so bad."

They drove on in silence to the police station. Trust or not, Willow was very aware of the fact that she was glad he was beside her.

The police station was busy. With phones ringing and voices rising over the din, Willow watched a detective take fingerprints off of the real estate papers. Many were smudged and unreadable, but a few were lifted intact. They took both Willow's and Rockford's prints, too, for comparison, since they had both handled the forms. They made photocopies, and gave Willow back the originals. Willow was impressed with their efficiency.

"The tow with the Burnetts' truck is here, sir," a young officer said to Detective Dunn. "They're pulling it around back."

The officer rose to his feet. "I don't suppose you'd want to come with me." He was smiling at the eager look on Willow's face. She looked like a racehorse, straining to win.

"Come on," he said, grinning. "Look at the truck."

They followed him out the back door of the station. The rain had stopped. An aged flatbed truck had pulled into the lot. The Burnetts' well-used truck was perched on it, slanted at a strange angle. The driver's side of the truck has been smashed in, and the front light and panel were squished like an accordion. The whole side of the truck was encrusted in mud.

The detectives were scurrying around, going over the

truck. They pulled out a white take-out food bag, and an empty cardboard coffee cup. Both bore the emblem DAN-CIN' JOE'S.

"We'll dust them for prints, but I don't think we'll get any good prints. And we can't be sure they have anything to do with the disappearance."

"Of course they do," added Willow. "Dancin' Joe's sure isn't the kind of place that the Burdetts would go to. It's a rough country bar up north of the city. Whoever stole that truck ate that food, you can be sure of that."

"And of course, you know that for a fact," snarled one of the detectives who was labeling the evidence in a plastic bag.

"Careful, partner," Rockford cautioned the detective with a grin, as he saw the tightness in Willow's jaw. "You're getting ready to dance with a porcupine."

The man sauntered off.

Opening the passenger door of the truck, Willow slipped into the cab. The worn vinyl of the seat reminded her of the Burdetts—hardworking, dependable. She felt her eyes get moist but pushed the emotion away.

The keys were in the ignition, as they had been when the truck was found. Fingerprinting dust was everywhere, left behind by the technicians who had collected the prints. Willow's hand shot out and started the engine. It leapt to life.

"Hey," called Dunn, stepping quickly to the door. "What are you doing?"

"Just seeing if it starts." Willow heard the engine running, but she heard something else, too. The radio in the truck had turned on with the ignition, and a country tune was blending in with the engine noise. "Boot-Scootin' Boogie" was piped into the truck. Willow smiled, and turned the key again, silencing the truck and the radio. She slipped out of the seat.

"Come on, Rockford, we're done here," she said cheerfully, waving good-bye to the detectives. "We'll leave
these gentlemen to waste all the time they want."

"Willow . . . keep cool. They're doing their job."

"They should have done their job yesterday. Then
maybe we'd know where the Burdetts are—and if they're
okay."

He took her arm, and quickly escorted her around the
building toward the car, before she could make a scene. He
held the real estate envelope tightly under his arm.

"Nice legs," one of the detectives said under his breath
with a low whistle, watching Willow's retreat.

"But what a mouth," said Detective Dunn, with a punch.
They went back to work.

"I can't believe they're just going to wait around for
that stupid Porter Blank to come back tomorrow," Willow
growled under her breath as they left the police station in
her Miata.

"Stupid Porter Blank—nice judgment. I didn't realize
you knew the man well enough to make an assessment like
that."

Willow gave a guilty smile as she shifted gears. "Point
well taken, counselor. Maybe the guy's a regular doll. I
don't know, since I've never met him. But to get involved
with Charley Morse . . ."

"I have to admit I don't know Porter too well myself.
I'm the new kid in town. Why don't we just wait and see?
Maybe there's a simple explanation for this whole thing."

"If there's a simple explanation, I'm going to find it."
Her jaw took on a determined look again.

"Why don't you let the cops do their job, Willow?
They're going to check out the prints, they're checking out
Morse, Porter will be back tomorrow. It's not their fault
that nobody knows where he went."

"Waiting until tomorrow may be a disaster if those two nice old people are in trouble."

She was chewing on her lower lip, and Rockford felt the tightening in his gut again. How could she do this to him, without even trying? "We've got no choice, Willow. We've got to wait. How about going to dinner with me tonight? If we do something distracting, the time will go faster."

The words were out of his mouth before his brain had a chance to censor them. He braced himself, waiting for the rejection that he knew would come.

"Okay."

"Okay? You'll go out with me? Tonight?" His heart beat faster.

"Yep. We do have to pass the time. But I have a few conditions. I get to pick the place, and the suit has to go. You have to change your clothes, okay?"

He would have agreed if she had asked him to jump to the moon.

"Do city slickers own a pair of jeans? How about a flannel shirt? Boots?"

"Not on your life."

They had pulled up to the curb at the real estate office. "Well, pardner, this country bumpkin has a hankering to go out with a cowboy tonight. Jeans, or no date."

Her laughing eyes met his, and all of a sudden his heart felt light. Heck, he had milked a cow. He could certainly get a pair of jeans.

"I've got this sudden urge to buy a pair of jeans. Can't figure out why."

"The department store in the shopping center might be a good place to start," she offered as they climbed out of the car. "I've got to do some paperwork at the office. Can you pick me up at my place at six? I live in the cottage behind the barn at Higher Horizons Farm. It's right down the road from the Burdetts' place.''

"I'll be there. In my jeans." He grinned, feeling like a boy waiting for Christmas.

"Make sure you're hungry, cowboy." She waved good-bye and walked toward the office door. "By the way, can you dance?"

"Like Fred Astaire."

"That should be a sight."

"So where are we going?" He thought of the wild and sophisticated clubs he had frequented in his New York past. He couldn't picture such a place existing here.

"We're going to Dancin' Joe's, out on the highway. You'll love it."

He thought of the take-out trash the police had found in the Burdetts' truck. DANCIN' JOE'S, it had said. "Willow, what are you up to?"

"I'm going to Dancin' Joe's tonight with you or without you. Like I told you . . . I don't like to wait. Are you coming?"

He hesitated for a minute, staring into the deepness of her eyes. "See you at six, cowgirl. Somebody's got to see that you stay out of trouble."

He was rewarded with a radiant smile. "Don't forget the jeans, city boy!"

He watched her disappear into the office, and took a deep breath. Jeans. Since the rain had stopped, he decided to walk the few blocks to the shopping center. He was amazed to hear himself whistling on the way.

Chapter Ten

He sure looked good in jeans. Willow suppressed a grin as she glanced at him while they were climbing into his car. The jeans were molded to him as if they had a right to be there. A pair of boots peeked out from under them. He wore a plaid flannel shirt, the vibrant red and green eye-catching under the tan suede jacket he wore.

"So do I pass inspection, Ms. Blake?" His eyes were twinkling, and the crooked smile that lit up his face made her melt. She laughed out loud. "You caught me looking at you. You look great. Right off the range. Rockford Cowpoke."

"Wait," he exclaimed, reaching into the backseat of the car. "This is the best." He pulled out a worn tan cowboy hat, plopped it on his head, and, pushing it back, gave her a cocky grin.

Her eyes got bigger. "Amazing. But that hat's not new."

"I bought it used at the saddlery. I thought it would make me seem more . . . real. Like I fit in. When we start asking questions. Thought I'd show you you're not the only clever person around here!"

Willow was impressed.

He started up the gray sedan, noticing Willow looking around the car.

"You don't like the car? I promise I'll drive carefully."

"It's not that. It's just that this car doesn't seem to . . . fit you."

The car had several years' wear on it, and was a neutral color, with stiff vinyl seats. It simply didn't match the silk-suited lawyer she had taken to the barn the day before.

"You make quite a detective, Willow. It's not mine—it's a rental. I didn't bring a car with me when I moved here a few weeks ago. I didn't bring much. Things were not good at home." She saw a look of pain cross his face.

Willow raised a palm toward him. "Stop. Sorry I was prying. I just figured you for a fancy foreign car. You know, like a Lamborghini or something."

His face looked shocked. "It's okay. I must be a caricature or something. My car is a Lamborghini. What color?"

She thought for a moment. "Silver," she said, squinting. "With a fantastic sound system."

He smiled meekly and nodded his head. "I guess I'm a predictable cuss, huh? No surprises." He started the car, and his face looked sad.

She had seen the look only seconds before when he had mentioned home. She didn't know the cause of the pain that seemed to envelop him at certain moments, but she wanted to erase it.

She reached out a hand, and touched his arm gently. He looked at her uncertainly.

"The hat, cowboy," she said with a wink. "The hat was a pleasant surprise. I love it."

He took a deep breath and smiled. "I can't believe it. I'm looking forward to going to Dancin' Joe's."

They headed for the highway.

The parking lot was well lit, and filled to the brink with pickup trucks, vans, and assorted cars. Dancin' Joe's had a big Saturday night crowd. They parked off to the side, hearing the twang of guitars and the beat of drums well before they even reached the door.

Rockford watched Willow stride confidently before him. She was dressed in a western jacket, with an abundance of fringe down the arms. She wore a plaid shirt with white mother-of-pearl buttons, over a short tiered jean skirt. About a mile of long, shapely leg could be viewed from under the skirt, her legs ending in hand-stitched cowgirl boots. Her short blond hair was worn soft and wispy, and her face was glowing with life.

She amazed him, the way she could switch styles and clothes as easy as turning channels on the TV, and still always look comfortable. She looked like she belonged in boots and fringe, the same way she had looked like she belonged in the wispy yellow chiffon he had first seen her wear.

He took her elbow as he opened the heavy wooden door. They had arrived at Dancin' Joe's.

They were immediately engulfed in a fog of cigarette smoke. Ears rang as the electric guitars vibrated in the air, cutting through the smoke and raucous racket of happy customers. They pushed their way through the mingling customers, and headed for the bar.

Waitresses dressed in sequined cowgirl outfits held trays high above their heads as they deftly stepped through the crowd, delivering drinks to couples seated at small round tables, or standing around the room in groups. Miraculously, Rockford found them two seats at the bar, recently vacated by a couple who had joined the dancers on the wooden floor in the center of the room.

"Not quite New York, eh, cowboy?" Willow asked with a grin. Two bearded guys were arm wrestling farther down the bar.

"Amazing. I wouldn't even know how to describe it."

"It's an adventure. Enjoy it. We'll just hang around, try to fit in."

Rockford looked around skeptically. "Well, anything's possible. What are you drinking?"

"Order a beer—or a beer, if you want to fit in. This isn't the Hilton. I'm having a Coke."

"Have to keep a clear head around me, Willow? Alcohol might make you give in to your feelings?" He was joking, but Willow's eyes met his, and he could see she was serious.

"I saw enough of what alcohol could do when I was a kid. It's not for me. I never touch the stuff. But you can order whatever you'd like, it doesn't bother me."

It was another clue to the mystery of Willow Blake, and he took it in stride without asking pressing questions.

One of the bartenders was heading their way.

"Two Cokes," Rockford said softly.

"Two Cokes for the teetotalers at the end," the gruff man yelled. They both winced.

"You don't have to drink soda on my account," she said after a minute.

"Maybe I do. Maybe it's my own feelings I ought to keep a clear head about. Besides," he said with a crooked grin, "I don't care for beer, and I doubt they carry my expensive brand of Scotch in this place."

The Cokes were plopped down unceremoniously in front of them, and the bartender disappeared. They drank in silence.

"We're probably the only customers in this joint who are drinking soda." Willow laughed, glancing around.

"So much for fitting in."

"Oh, don't worry about it. There's other ways of fitting in and meeting people." She was standing suddenly, and taking him by the arm.

Willow was heading for the dance floor, where boots were flying, heels were clicking, and dozens of dancers were moving to the beat.

"That's what I'm afraid of," he grumbled as she led

him onto the floor. "This is an adventure that could put me in traction."

But she smiled up at him, and he decided to give it a try.

The band was starting a new song; the guitars twanged, setting Rockford's nerves on edge. Willow led him to the edge of the dance crowd.

"Just try to follow along. This is a popular country dance song."

"Boot-Scootin' Boogie" was reverberating through the smoky room, and the dancing crowd went into action, heels clacking in unison, bodies moving to the well-choreographed pattern of the song. At least most of the bodies were moving. Rockford was horrified.

"They're all doing the same steps," he whispered in anguish, as he watched the flying feet around him. Willow was moving with the crowd with grace and ease. He stared at her with suspicion. "You know how to do these steps, don't you? You tricked me."

He was trying to follow Willow's feet, but his mind didn't seem to be working quickly enough. He turned the wrong way and ran right into a tiny brunette dancer.

"Ow, cowboy. Watch your turns!"

He turned and glowered at Willow, who by this time was laughing out loud.

"Don't you New Yorkers know how to dance?" she teased, seeing his exasperated look.

Again he tried to follow the crowd. Right, left, turn. This time he backed into a big bearded man.

"Get your feet going the right way, buster, or we're going to have to take this outside."

Rockford grabbed Willow's arm. "You're going to have to send me to dancing school before I'm willing to take on

Brutus back there. I'm finished. I'll wait at the bar. This was a failure.''

"It was perfect. Sit at the bar and wait, and see what you can find out. Watch what happens here, because I'll be doing the same.''

He shook his head, and reclaimed his bar stool.

The song ended seconds after he left, and instantly, several men were standing around Willow.

"Nice dancing, babe,'' a youngish man said, his shaggy blond hair reaching over his shirt collar. He was looking her over appreciatively. He made her skin crawl, but she smiled back. The band started a new song, slower, the kind you dance with a partner.

"How about a dance?'' propositioned the blond. "I can promise you your feet will remain intact dancing with me, instead of that clod you came in with.''

"Oh, he's a great guy,'' she said with a smile. "He just needs dance lessons. He's from the city.''

The blond one nodded, as if that explained everything. He held out his arm for a dance, and Willow went toward him, swaying to the music. On the bar stool, Rockford bit his lip, watching. What was she up to?

"So are you a real cowbody, or just dressed up for dancing?'' she whispered in her partner's ear.

"I'm a real country boy, ma'am. Herb's the name. What's your name? I haven't seen you around here before.''

"I'm, uh, Willa,'' she said softly. "It's my first time here. How about horses? Do you ride? Live on a farm?''

"I spend some time on farms. I live in an apartment right now, until I get my life in order.''

"I have friends who have a farm—horses, cows, the whole works. I like to visit there. Maybe you know them. The Burdetts? They live out on Old Silo Road.''

"Never heard of them. Come on, let's make the most out of this dance. You're a great-looking girl."

He pulled her closer, wrapping a muscled arm around her back. Her chest was crushed into his; she could feel his thighs pressed against hers. Her stomach began to roll as he tightened his grip.

"Uh, I've got to excuse myself," she said quickly, pulling away. "Little girls' room. You know how these things are." She took off across the smoke-filled room, leaving him to shake his shaggy blond head. He turned his attention to a redhead with braids who was sitting alone at a table.

Willow felt a sense of relief as she escaped. She did go to the ladies' room, to wash her hands, and dampen her face, as if to remove the feeling of his hands touching her. She was totally grossed out, and had gained no information for her trouble. She had to try another tack.

The tiny brunette who had been practically stepped on by Rockford in the dance line came into the ladies' room, stopping at the mirror to reapply her abundance of makeup.

"That's some hunk you're with," the brunette said, making confirmation as she pushed her face close to the mirror. "What's his name?"

"Uh, Rocky. He's Rocky."

"Too bad he can't dance."

"He'll learn. He's new around here."

"So are you. You're not a regular here. Where'd you learn how to dance like that? You're pretty good." The brunette looked envious.

"Oh, I've been around. Thought I'd try a new place. You're pretty good yourself."

"Well, thanks. Lots of strangers around here lately. It's getting to be some kind of trend, this country dance stuff. But some of us have done it forever, you know?"

"Ever run into a stranger named Charley Morse? Kind of a tough guy, little bit of a New York accent?"

The brunette narrowed her eyes. ''What's somebody like you looking for somebody like Charley Morse? You'd be better off sticking to that klutzy cowboy you got there. Safer.''

Willow's heart began to beat. ''You know Charley? Can you tell me how to find him?''

''Not on your life. Not on *my* life. Forget it. Just go teach your cowboy how to dance, before somebody does it for you.''

She turned on the heel of her well-worn boot, and scooted out the door, leaving only the scent of her perfume behind.

Willow left the confines of the ladies' room, and headed toward Rockford, who was still perched on his stool. The two men near him were still arm wrestling, swigging on drinks between each bout, and looking wilder by the minute. Soon it would be a contest to see who could remain on the stool longer. Rockford watched them curiously, amazed.

She had almost reached his side, when the burly, bearded man who had objected to Rockford's erratic dancing stepped directly into her way.

Well over six feet in height, and topping the scale at close to three hundred pounds, he was definitely a presence. Having seen him on the dance floor, she knew he was surprisingly light and coordinated on his feet for such a giant guy.

''Been looking for you, Blondie. How about dancing next to a real man?'' He shrugged over his shoulder toward Rockford insultingly.

''That's okay, I'm done dancing for now. He's not so bad; he just needs dance lessons.''

Out of the corner of her eye, she could see Rockford grimace.

''Come on, baby, let's take a turn.'' Another slow song

was playing, and that would mean dancing close again, and Willow didn't think she could handle it. Intimacy was tough, but with strangers like this, it was simply unbearable. He was running his hand up her arm, playing with the fringe on her jacket.

She pulled her arm away. "Listen, I said no. I'm getting ready to leave. Thanks anyway."

He grabbed her arm as she tried to step around him. "Not so fast, little lady. Didn't your daddy teach you manners?"

She spun on her heel and faced him, her face showing rage. Rockford jumped to his feet, rushing toward her.

Willow stood her ground. "My daddy taught me that men like you and him are the scum of the earth. Now let go of my arm before I have to hurt you."

He put back his head and laughed out loud, still holding her arm in his tight grip.

Willow didn't hesitate. She pulled back her right arm and threw a punch at his face, catching him right below the eye. He yelped in pain and lessened his grip, and she broke away, right into Rockford's arm. He spun her around, pushing her toward the door. A crowd had started to gather.

It didn't take long for the bearded bully to catch his breath. He reached out and caught Rockford by the collar of his jacket.

Rockford turned and faced the drunk man. He could clearly see the spot where Willow's punch had landed. The guy was going to have a shiner. Rockford smiled.

"What are you smiling at, you cow pile? You oughtta teach that woman some manners. Nobody hits me and gets away with it." The burly man pulled back his arm, ready to pulverize his prey. Rockford's reflexes went into action.

He might not know how to dance, and he might currently be out of shape a bit. But he and Peter hadn't played college soccer for nothing, and when push came to shove, he knew he had a great outside kick.

As the big fist came toward him, he ducked and pulled his leg back. He delivered a blow right at the bully's knee, and he crumpled into a pile on the floor.

Instantly, he headed for the door, but the two arm wrestlers had miraculously stood up from their stools and blocked his path. Each put a hand on his shoulders, and he had a feeling that his minutes of comfort were over.

He looked from one angry face to another.

"You kicked our buddy, mister." The tension in the air was thick.

All of a sudden, Willow was at his elbow, smiling gaily.

"He sure did, and you should thank him. That guy is no friend of yours. That bully was just telling me that you two must really like each other, since you were sitting their holding hands all night. Now that's an insult. But I told him I didn't believe it."

She gave the two men a perky smile. They evaluated her words though their haze of alcohol.

"He's insulting our manhood, and you stood up for us. Thanks, man." The clamped hands released, patting Rockford's shoulders. "We'll take care of him."

Willow grabbed Rockford's arm, and pulled him out the door, while havoc broke loose in the bar behind them. You could hardly hear the band over the din.

They gulped in the fresh air as they ran across the parking lot, and sped off into the night.

"Well, is that what you call an adventure? In my book, that was a big failure," Rockford remarked as they sped down the highway.

"Not really. I talked to a woman who knew Charley Morse. But she wouldn't talk about him. We'll have to make a new plan."

They rode in silence, totally unaware of the conversation

that was going on in the dark corner of the bar they had just left.

"Who were those two troublemakers?" the man who sat in shadows said.

"Her name is Willa," said the blond man with scraggy hair. "I tried to dance with her, but she just kept talking."

"What did she talk about?"

"She just wanted to know if I was a real cowboy. If I knew friends of hers who had horses, named Burdett or something. Then she ran off to the bathroom."

"Who else did she talk to?"

"They weren't here that long. The guy can't dance to save his life. She came out of the bathroom with Carla. Maybe she talked to her."

"Get her. Quick."

Carla came, her face dark and worried. She answered his questions.

"She didn't say where she was from. Said she wanted to try a new dance place. Said her guy's name was Rocky. Then she asked about you."

The man's face froze. "What did you say?"

Carla's heart started to hammer. "Nothing. Nothing," she lied. "I told her I never heard of any Charley Morse. That's all."

He dismissed her. He turned to the man on his right. "Find out who they are, and why they came here. We can't afford to have them ruin things at this date."

He stood to go, and people started scurrying to do his bidding.

"This time tomorrow, I want answers, or else. Understood?"

Several heads nodded. He'd get the answers he wanted, no matter what.

Chapter Eleven

Willow arrived at the office early the next morning. Even at the early hour, the heat of the sun was promising a warm summer day. Spring would soon be a memory. She threw herself into her work, coffee mug in hand. At 2:00 P.M. she had a date with the elusive Mr. Porter Blank, and she planned to do a lot of work before then.

Gail arrived, with a smile, to tackle the phones, which began to ring promptly at 8:30. It was the busy time of year in the world of real estate. Clients who were thinking of selling were calling for property appraisals. Buyers were eagerly seeking information on offerings that they had seen in newspaper ads, or on properties they had seen with sale signs strategically placed in front yards.

Mildred had entered the door shortly after Gail, quietly perching at her desk and getting right to work. The receptionist forwarded calls to Willow and Mildred alternately, and a very workable flow developed.

The mailman plopped a stack of letters on Gail's desk midmorning, which Willow sifted through quickly. Disappointingly, the stack contained necessary but unexciting mail, and not the miracle she had been hoping for—a letter or card from the Burdetts, saying they were all right.

The phones had stilled for a minute, and in the lull, Willow spoke.

"We make a pretty good team here," she said to Gail and Mildred. "I've got four appointments for listings, and three families who want to see properties. If this keeps up, Mr. Reynolds is going to be able to retire!''

Mildred laughed. ''He's going to be thrilled when he gets home next week. I think I've got a buyer for that Northway house, full price and a quick close. And several appointments for listings, too. Our ads are really doing well. You have quite good timing on the telephone, Gail. I don't know what we would do without you right now.''

Gail blushed, glad to be appreciated. ''Thanks. I love it here. You guys are great to work with, and the customers are nice . . . except for that charming Mr. Morse the other day, I might add.''

''Listen, Gail,'' Willow said seriously. ''If that man ever calls again, do everything you can to get a telephone number, address, anything. I'd do just about anything to make sure the Burdetts are okay.''

Gail nodded, as the phones began to ring again.

The bar was dark, even though the sun blazed brightly outside. Only one or two customers at a time graced the bar. An older guy in white pants, T-shirt, and apron swept the floor, laboriously moving chairs and small round tables, collecting the trash and debris from the busy night before.

Dancin' Joe's was almost silent during the day. An aged jukebox stood in the corner, occasionally playing a country tune, but the volume was turned down low, and the music was just a hint of sound in the air.

Back in the corner, underneath the beam of a dangling overhead light constructed from a wagon wheel, two men sat huddled over a small table. Body language said it all— one was angry, and one was scared.

''The car was a rental, Mr. Morse. It's been out for several weeks now.''

''So who's leasing the stupid car, brainless? Did you

think getting that information would tell us what we need to know? Go look at the lease.''

The thin blond man swallowed hard. ''But I did, sir. I got the name. But it didn't give me any answers.'' He winced as he finished his words, as if he expected a blow to come. There was only silence.

''The name?'' The angry man was barely controlling his rage.

''It's a nun, sir. Sister George from St. Francis Parish. A nun rented the car, but that blond was no nun.''

A quizzical look replaced the anger on the older man's face. ''How do you like that? They were driving a sister's car. Gotta be a reason for that. Go ask at St. Francis. Find this Sister George. And find that blond. That nervy broad is no nun. A looker like that can't hide in a town this size. What was her name again?''

''Willa. Carla said she said her name was Willa.''

''Willa. Willa.'' His beady eyes showed he was thinking. ''Nervy Willa.'' His eyes became like slits. ''I know one nervy broad in this town. I wonder . . .''

He shot some orders at the young man, who was relieved to be off the hook temporarily, and given another job. The blond sped out the door, his worn boots punching the wooden floor as he left.

A phone call came in less than twenty minutes later. The young man had followed orders, and his hunch had proven right. He had sent the young cowboy to scope out Reynolds Realty in town, and to call and describe the only nervy broad he knew in Ryerstown—Willow Blake. Tall and blond and gorgeous, he had reported. And nervy.

He had picked the realtor at random, basically because her office was directly across the street from old Porter. She only had to file papers, and collect a huge commission. What greedy realtor in the world wouldn't flip for a deal like that? He had picked her, but he had picked wrong.

Why had the long-legged blond showed up at Dancin' Joe's, asking about him, and giving a phony name? She smelled something wrong with the deal, and he had far too much at stake to risk any problems. How had she found him at Dancin' Joe's? And why? Low profile was his strong point. The people he worked for hired him on the strength of it.

A feeling of nervousness found its way to the pit of his stomach, boring a hole in him, like a bug in a rotted tree. He had to do some thinking about this Willow/Willa broad. This whole deal hinged on timing. He needed a day or two, that was all, but it was crucial. He couldn't afford to make a stink, not when he was halfway through the plan. He'd have to find a way to deter her, without making trouble. Darn blonds, anyway. They were always more trouble than they were worth.

How about the guy who was with her? He had two left feet, and drove a nun's car. Not much to go on. The stomach was rumbling now. He tossed the feeling away with a long swig of Scotch. Charley Morse had a problem, but he'd handle it without getting the top brass upset. He had to. Problem solvers were supposed to solve problems, not make them.

Another swig of Scotch chased the first down his throat. He started to feel better, watching the old man sweep the floor in front of him, cleaning up problems.

Willow was on time for her scheduled appointment with Porter Blank at 2:00 in the afternoon, wearing a beige linen suit, with heels, the real estate portfolio tucked efficiently under her arm. Prudence greeted her at the entryway, escorting her to Mr. Porter's office. There was no sign of Rockford.

"Ah, Ms. Blake, come in." The man who rose from an immense cherry wood desk was smiling. She judged him in an instant. He was approximately fifty, in fairly good shape but with a slight paunch, hair graying around the temples to give him a seasoned look. His suit was expensive; his shoes were hidden behind the desk. She focused on his eyes.

His face might be smiling, but his eyes were troubled. Whoever had coined the phrase "the eyes are the windows of the soul" had said a mouthful. If she was looking into the soul of Mr. Porter, there was a storm a-brewing. The man was under stress.

"It's great to finally meet you, sir," she said politely, extending her hand. His handshake was too gentle, his skin moist and clammy. "I have received real estate papers about the ten-acre Burdett property, listing you as power of attorney. It's a rather unorthodox deal."

"Is there something not in order? Did you have questions?"

His eyes were darting now, reminding her of a frog before it zaps a fly. She had no intention of being zapped.

"I have a bookful of questions. You see, I happen to know that the Burdetts were very much against selling. Suddenly, these papers appear, and the Burdetts disappear. I wanted to understand what took place."

"People change their minds, Ms. Blake. The buyer offered an amazing sum of money. The Burdetts sold. They've probably taken off to celebrate their good fortune. I'm sure I don't know why you are making such a big deal about this."

"The police have located their truck. They also consider the Burdetts missing."

"The truck was probably left behind when they left, and stolen from the empty property. Certainly unfortunate, but certainly a sign of our uneasy times. Again, I assure you, the real estate deal is proper and settled and was accepted by all parties involved."

She started to speak, but the well-modulated voice of the

lawyer continued. "The title search has been completed, fees paid, the proper documents signed and countersigned. All that is needed is for you to sign the said documents and deliver them to the courthouse, then make out a bill for your services and fee. I will pay you immediately." He held up his hand when she attempted to speak again.

"Please, Ms. Blake. I can see that you are concerned about the Burdetts, but I simply do not have time to make a federal case out of a simple real estate transaction. I assure you that I will contact you immediately when I hear from the couple, to allay your worries. But as far as I am concerned, the deal is completed, and Mr. Morse is the owner of the farm." He stood, and offered his weak handshake again.

Willow was fuming. She kept her hands at her side as she stood and looked at him.

"The papers may be in order, Mr. Blank. But the people are not in order. You may consider this deal finished, but I disagree. Mr. Morse may take possession of the farm, but I won't go away. I'm not going to drop this until I see for myself that the Burdetts are all right."

She turned on her heel and stomped into the hallway, where Prudence was sitting at her desk. She fought back the tears that threatened to take up residence in her eyes. She would not cry. She would not give up. "Is Mr. Harrison here, Prudence?" she asked.

"Do you have an appointment?" Prudence began, but then she saw the ferocious look in Willow's eyes. "Well, um, he's not here today. He had some personal matters to take care of. Would you care to leave a message?"

Willow took the offered notepad and left a message. "Deterred but not defeated. Call me. Willow." Prudence looked at the words, and soundlessly put the note into Rockford's message slot, watching the determined blond stomp out the door. Young women were certainly different today. Strong-minded. Self-sufficient. Suddenly Prudence smiled sadly. She wished that she could will away twenty years from her age, to live like today's young women.

But then the phone rang, its muted sound cutting into her thought. "Law offices. Can I help you . . . I see. Do you have an appointment?" She grimaced at herself, efficiently putting the client's time in the book, as the phone rang again.

Rockford was exhausted. He had spent the better part of the day at the bank, in the company of the indefatigable Sister George. By the time the paper shuffling was done, the little manipulator had relieved him of sixty thousand dollars, and he was a proud trustee of the new Ryerstown AIDS Support Fund. How the number had leaped up to the extra ten thousand dollars, he had no idea, except that he had learned from past experience with the inimitable Georgina Harrison that she usually got what she wanted.

And it did make him feel good, helping someone. Peter used to harp on him about that. Peter would be proud. Heck, he was proud himself. But he was tired. After leaving the bank, he had gone home and slipped into sweats, forcing himself to take a long, hard jog. He felt an unfamiliar wave of restlessness flowing over him, making him unsettled and tense.

Several miles later, he felt calmer, but drained.

Back at the apartment, he had called the office, and had received Willow's message. Back in his "official clothes," he climbed back into the rental car and drove into town to see Willow. The closer he got to the real estate office, the better he felt. He felt a pull to Willow that he couldn't understand. There was absolutely nothing calming or gentle about the woman, but he was driven to her by a force he couldn't identify.

He saw her the moment he walked in the door. There

was a yellow pencil stuck behind one ear, and a phone was plastered to the other. The remains of a fast-food lunch were spread across her desk.

She looked up as he entered and she smiled, hanging up the phone. That smile filled his heart, filled his soul. The restlessness flowed away, effortlessly, and he felt peace.

"Hi, Blondie." He gave her a crooked smile.

"So where were you, counselor, when I needed you? I had to tackle Porter Blank myself. He's a slimy thing, you know."

"I was at the bank. It's a long story. I don't know Porter well myself, but I'll take your character reference as gospel, if you'll go to dinner with me."

She cleared the debris from her desk with a swipe, filling the trash can. "Best offer I've had all day." She stood, wiggling her feet around under her desk to retrieve her shoes.

His heart felt light.

"I'm out of here, Gail," she said to the receptionist. "Leave any messages on my home machine, okay? I'll see you tomorrow."

Gail smiled in agreement, as the two went out the door, arm in arm.

Willow felt a surge of happiness, of completeness as they stepped onto the sidewalk. The good feelings ended abruptly.

"My car," she whined.

"We'll take whatever car you want, crazy lady."

"No," she whined louder. *"My car!"* He looked at the Miata then, parked as usual by the curb. The black convertible roof was slit viciously across the top in a crisscross manner. Pointed strips of ruined vinyl hung down into the interior.

They looked at each other for a silent moment. Random vandalism or pointed message? The good feelings had ebbed away.

Chapter Twelve

Willow pulled her portable phone out of her bag, and called the police. Detective Dunn took down the information glumly. The police made arrangements to meet at Willow's house. "I can't leave the car here in town; it might rain."

So in the end, they took both cars, Willow driving the Miata, and Rockford following in his rental.

When the police arrived, she gave the information for the police report. She contacted her auto insurance agent. She felt violated and angry. He helped her haul a blue waterproof tarp from the barn, draping it over the forlorn Miata to protect it from the elements.

Rockford had followed her into the little cottage at the back of the farm. He felt a bit like a useless appendage as he watched her competently handle the details of the vandalism. But despite her control, he could see she was upset and he had a strong urge to comfort her. What would she think if he crossed the small room and enveloped her in his arms?

She'd push him away. He didn't doubt it for a minute. So he pushed the thought away, instead. Willow Blake was a mystery. She was a complicated, intense person, and he was drawn to her with an intensity that amazed him. When it came to Willow, he was a little like a rat caught in a maze, with no map, no compass. Uncharted territory.

He smiled to himself. Maybe they just needed time. She

was worth it. He sat back, and waited for her to make the first move.

Willow had been busy on the phone, but Rockford's presence hadn't been out of her mind for an instant. He sat across the room, quiet and attentive. It was mesmerizing, she thought suddenly, how he filled the room. He was a big man, broad shoulders, long legs. But it was more than that. It was his presence, his personality. She felt a tingle travel her spine like an electric current through a hot wire.

"Thanks for your patience. This has made me a little crazy."

"No problem," he said softly. "Done the phone calls?"

"Police, insurance, and ordered a replacement top from a friend. They'll get it up here by tomorrow." She was biting her lip, deep in thought. She stood with her back to him, staring out the window.

"Was it just random vandalism? Or do you think it was a warning, Rockford? Do you think somebody's trying to intimidate me to stop looking for the Burdetts?"

"I don't know. So are you intimidated?"

She turned and grinned. "Don't know the word, counselor. But it's interesting that someone would try . . . I can't stop, though, no matter what."

He nodded, watching the way her eyes flashed when she was thinking. He stood up suddenly, trying to fight the wave of emotion that was suddenly roaring in him like an August forest fire, uncontrollable, unquenchable. She was gorgeous, she was so brave and so alive, and he wanted her more than anything in his life. But he was afraid she wouldn't feel the same.

She saw him stand, saw him looking at her, heeding the fact that the room had gotten even noticeably smaller. She swallowed hard. Rockford Farquahar Harrison III was a man to be reckoned with. Her pulse was hammering as she watched him from across the small room. His strong jawline was offset by the look of vulnerability in his eyes. His strong shoulders were noticeably tense. He was knockdown gorgeous, and he didn't even know it.

Willow had come to an emotional crossroads as she stood there absorbing the unspoken messages that flashed like current between them.

Pull back, sever the feelings, said one of the voices in her head. *You can't trust a man . . . you can't let yourself be vulnerable.*

But it's Rockford, strong and true, answered another of the voices. *You can learn to trust. . . .*

She watched the fine, hard lines of his face, and knew that he was watching her. He knew. He stood there, watching the silent battle that went on in her head, and let her work it out. No coercion, no impatience, no self-doubt. Her heart swelled at that realization, filled with a strange and humbling emotion that was totally new. It was love. She drew in a deep long breath, her eyes locked with his, feeling her knees begin to tremble.

His eyes were warm, and encouraging, but he didn't say a word. He just watched her. It was up to her, she realized. He was giving her the power to choose.

He was giving her freedom, and by that very allowance, he had captured her heart. She could trust this man.

Her heart was hammering in her chest as she took a step toward him, raising her arms. He smiled, his face lighting up with feeling, and opened his arms to her, and she flowed to him, like a flower to the sun.

They fit. He enveloped her tall, slim body, tucking her into his, and held her close. She could feel her own heart hammering, and after a moment, could feel his. He was warm and solid, and as they stood there, holding each other, not even moving, she realized an amazing thing.

Instead of the usual feeling of losing something of herself when she got close to a person, the exact opposite was happening. Instead of feeling like she was giving up her personhood, her self of personal power that she had worked so hard to develop, she felt a new sense of power flowing into her. She felt stronger, more alive, as they touched, as if a distinct energy was flowing from one to the other.

She pulled her head back in amazement, and met the eyes she sought, drinking in their message like a weary desert traveler finding refreshing water. He was holding her, Willow Blake, and she was okay. He wasn't trying to coerce her, to correct her, to change her, to mold her. He liked who she was. His very acceptance of her opened the floodgates of feeling as she stood looking into his eyes. The feeling was very, very mutual.

She tilted her head slightly, opening her lips, her hands around his neck gently pulling him toward her. He didn't need a second invitation. His mouth touched hers, softly at first. She kissed him right back. She heard soft gasps in the silence of the cottage, startled to realize they were coming from her.

"Ah, Willow, Willow," he groaned, pulling her close to him. "You are so special. I'll wait as long as it takes for you to trust me."

The phone rang.

The shrill noise cut through the air, and brought them rapidly back into the present. They both wanted to cling to the tender moment. But the phone couldn't be ignored. Too much was going on around them.

It was already the fourth ring by the time Willow reached the receiver.

"Thank goodness I caught you, Willow," came Gail's voice over the wire. The normally unflappable receptionist sounded tense, worried.

"What's going on, Gail?"

"I don't know. Maybe it's nothing. But I don't believe in coincidences. You have a message here, from Bill

Boylan at National Realty across town. It's about that Charley Morse, Willow. Seems our Mr. Morse has just approached him about purchasing a run-down farm for half a million dollars.''

''I don't get it. The Burdett deal is already done.''

''He asked about the Burdett deal, Willow, because he is suspicious of Morse, and he learned you filed the papers for the Burdett sale. It's *another* farm, Willow, on the same road, owned by a couple named Harris! Charley Morse is at it again.''

''Did he talk to the owners, Gail? Do they want to sell?'' A sick feeling was creeping up on her, and she knew what Gail's answer would be.

''They don't want to sell. I'm worried for them, Willow, especially since we still can't find the Burdetts.''

Willow took down the realtor's information and promised to call and look into it. A two-minute phone call with Bill Boylan proved her fears were justified. The couple refused to sell when Bill approached them, and Charley Morse had been furious on the phone when he had learned the news. Bill didn't have a number to reach him.

Willow hung up the phone, giving Rockford the unhappy news. The Harrises had to be warned and protected. And Charley Morse had to be stopped. She picked up the phone and called the police.

The day went downhill rapidly. The police reported that the Harris couple weren't taking the Morse offer seriously, and had declined any police protection, scoffing at the thought of being in danger.

No one could find the mysterious Charley Morse. There was no word from the Burdetts. The magical moments spent in Rockford's arms had been relegated to a happy memory, pushed aside by the worry they both felt about what was going on.

Driving to city hall, they had spent two fruitless hours combing local records. Why did Charley Morse want those decrepit farms? What was so special about them that he was willing to pay several times the market values, even coercing owners to sell? Why *those* farms, located so close to each other?

It was not good land for development. The rocky ground with bad runoff made it unsuitable for efficient septic systems, and there was no public sewer available so far from town. There had been no building permits, change of zoning petitions, or any other study filed which would indicate that the land was suitable or proposed for building of any kind.

They checked the records for any easements, either existing or proposed, that would mean alteration or use of the land by electric, water, gas, or telephone companies, rail lines or oil pipelines. No information existed.

Willow spoke to a local geologist, speculating on the possibility of some hidden value for the land that was not yet explored. Coal? Oil? Some other valuable minable mineral? The geologist had laughed, reassuring her that the area in question held no such secrets, and that the only thing that would be found under the depleted farmland was rock and more rock.

But why? Why did Charley Morse place such a value on those run-down farms? There were no answers to be found.

Willow and Rockford stopped for hamburgers and fries at the end of a long day, sitting across from each other in a well-worn leather booth at the local diner. It was an evening hangout spot for the local teenagers, and the corner jukebox was blasting out an alternative rock song at a decibel level that would challenge even the most insensitive ears.

Leaning across the table, they kept their heads together

to hear each other's words amid the din. Willow felt a rosy glow as she watched his face react when he told a story, laughing and dramatic. She began to get a feel for the man she cared so much about. His early life, growing up with all of the trappings a body could want, but feeling an emptiness that can only be filled by caring relationships.

He told her about Peter, vocalizing his feelings, his guilt, his pain at losing his best friend. He actually spoke aloud of the anger and rage that had built in him at Peter's death, and how he couldn't go on in the flawed justice system that let murderers like Marco Slergetti go free.

She listened. She nodded and acknowledged his words, but she didn't interrupt. She didn't soften his words with protests, trying to take the edge off his guilt. But she didn't condemn him either. She simply understood. And listened. He loved her for it.

She spoke later in halting tones of her own childhood, of the mean and negative man who had hurt her so badly in the name of fatherhood, and of her own struggle to find a new life. She shared stories about Maggie and the kids and demonstrated the sign language she was learning to communicate with a deaf child.

They held hands when they left the restaurant, and they walked a few blocks through town together, still entranced at the newness of having someone be so close.

Willow was amazed at herself and her reactions to this man. The night air was warm, but she shivered at the thought. Anticipation? He felt her tremor, and put an arm around her, pulling her close.

"Cold, Willow? Let's head for the car. How about stopping by my house before we head out to the farm? I want to check my messages."

She nodded, and climbed into the rental car wordlessly a few minutes later. He drove silently, lost in his own thoughts, pulling up to the white Victorian house.

"It's an apartment upstairs. The entrance is around back."

She followed him as he led, curious to see where he lived. She wanted to know about his life, what mattered to him, what he liked, what he thought. She wanted him. She swallowed hard at the thought.

His key opened the upstairs door easily, and he led her into a cute apartment, its big windows filled with plants, and cheerful colorful pillows tossed haphazardly on the couch.

"Just let me check my messages, and we'll go." He disappeared into another room, shutting the door behind him.

She decided to give herself a tour of the small apartment. The kitchen was clean and orderly, but it had a well-lived-in look. She noticed the rack of spices over the stove. Funny, Rockford hadn't struck her as much of a cook. There was so much she didn't know about him.

Crossing the living room, she was struck again by the color and warmth of the room. It didn't really match the man she had come to know, the man who wore silk shirts and had been suffering depression over the death of his friend.

On the other side of the living room she found the bathroom, its door halfway open. Thoughts had already been bombarding her mind, and as the bathroom came into view, the worst of her theories was proven true. With her mouth hanging open, she saw a sight that broke her heart, broke her trust.

It was laundry. Hanging demurely from the shower rod, from the towel rack, her eyes lighted on women's clothing. Pantyhose and underwear were drying innocently in the air.

A woman lived in this apartment. With Rockford. Bile rose in her throat, as remorse for her own foolishness swept over her. She had blindly trusted him, naively assumed that her values would be his, that he would be hers, as she longed to be his.

But he belonged to someone else, if not legally, at least ethically, by his living situation. And that kind of relationship was not acceptable to Wilhemina Blake. Ever.

She swallowed hard, mustering up the courage that had gotten her through many a tough day. She forced the tears to retreat from her eyes. Willow Blake would not cry over a man like this. Ever. It was the principle of the thing.

She turned softly on her heel, and walked noiselessly to the door of the apartment, letting herself out. She bounded down the steps, and around the building before she realized that she had no car. She took a deep breath, and hunched up her shoulders, moving quickly down the street. Three blocks later, a convenience store came into sight. She called Maggie. Maggie was coming to get her. She asked no questions, which was a good thing, because for once in her life, Willow Blake had absolutely no answers, no answers at all. Her heart was broken.

Chapter Thirteen

When Rockford came out of the bedroom a few minutes later, he was pulling a sweater over his head.

"Willow?"

The room was silent and empty. She was gone.

Where did she go? What spooked her? He looked quickly around the apartment, his eyes finally lighting on George's lingerie. She couldn't have thought . . . But anything was possible with the gun-shy Willow. He had never thought to tell her about George.

He got in his car, and began driving around the neighborhood. He tried to convince himself that maybe she had simply gone for a walk, but he knew it was more serious than that. Several minutes later, he drove by the convenience store a few blocks away, just in time to see her long legs disappear into a beat-up Suburban wagon. Maggie's wagon.

Well, she was safe, and on her way home. Though he had no idea of how to bring back the warmth and closeness they had felt all day. He remembered the sweet smell of her skin, the texture of her blond hair, the way her lips had opened to his. He wanted her, he needed her. One way or another, he would convince her of that. But for now, she was on her way home.

He climbed back up the stairs to the apartment, feeling defeated. After a few minutes, when she would have had time to get home, he dialed her number. The phone answered on the first ring. It was her answering machine.

"Hi, this is Willow. I'm not answering the phone right now. Please leave a message at the beep. Unless this is Rockford. In which case, don't bother. Ever."

He heard the beep, and left a message anyway. "This is Rockford. In this great country of ours, a man is innocent until *proven* guilty. Circumstantial evidence is thrown out in court. A person should have their day in court, Wilhemina. It's the principle of the thing. Call me, Willow. I love you." He hung up the phone, feeling sadness like a physical pain inside of him. He knew she wouldn't call. It was over.

At that instant, the door opened, and his sister George came bounding in, balancing a large box.

"Whoa, get this, big brother. The natives are restless."

He saved the carton, noticing the holes poked in its top. "Uh-oh, George, what's in here?"

She closed the door behind her, and opened the flaps of the box. Kittens. There were six to be exact. Two yellow tabbies, two black, two black-and-white. They scrambled to freedom, instantly scurrying to explore their environment.

Rockford was aware that he had developed a headache. "George?" he asked, rubbing his temples. "What are we doing with them?"

"Somebody was going to drown them, do you believe it? I can't stand by and have them drown. We'll have to find homes, that's all. Kinda cute, aren't they?" One was climbing the curtains, and one had already knocked over his stack of books.

"Adorable. Can we stuff them?"

"A wise guy. Now tell me what's wrong. You look like you lost your best friend."

Now that was a true thought. "She was here, she left. I think it was your underwear."

Georgina sized up the information in a flash. "Your girl-friend thought you were cohabiting, eh?"

"You know, for a nun, you are pretty obnoxious." He smiled at his sister, glad to see that she instantly understood.

"Well, she'll get over it. You just should have told her about me. It's the tall blond, right? The realtor? Willow Blake?"

"You know about her?"

"I know about everything. When are you going to learn that? But she's a quality person, so it'll take care of itself. Give her time. Now tell me about what's going on with you two. I can see she means something to you. She must be something special to have conquered the 'Knight of the Nightclub,' Mr. Rockford Farquahar Harrison III."

"I've changed, Georgina. You know that."

He sat in his chair, and she stepped behind him, her strong and compact hands kneading his tight shoulders as he talked. He told her about meeting Willow, about the real estate deal, the Burdetts, Charley Morse, the car, the farm, and his love for Willow. She listened patiently.

"Well, it's clear what you have to do."

He stared at her for a minute. "What? It's sure not clear to me."

"We have to go country line dancing."

His eyes opened wider. Was his sister losing it?

"What are you talking about, Georgina? This is serious."

"Don't challenge a nun. It isn't the least bit polite. Now listen, you big brute. What you need is a way to show Willow that you care about what she cares about, that you are willing to prove it to her. She likes country music and dancing. You have two left feet. Imagine her surprise if you learned to do a dance or two for her. And besides, I think there are more answers to be found at that club.

"You have to wait for her to calm down anyway. Why waste the time? She'd be tickled pink at the effort, I can assure you. I'll teach you to dance, and we can look over Dancin' Joe's one more time. Trust me."

"Well, your harebrained schemes often work out, I'll grant you that. Are you sure you know how to do country line dances?"

"Of course. I'm as good as Reba McEntire, didn't you know? I told you, I know *everything!*"

Within minutes, they had both changed into jeans, and were driving determinedly on the highway out of town, heading for Dancin' Joe's.

"I'm not sure this is such a hot idea, George. Last time I was here with Willow, some guys gave us a really hard time."

Georgina laughed, filling the car with the tinkling, happy sound. "Don't worry, Rockford. You have God on your side here. I've never met a cowboy I couldn't convert!"

Since it was the middle of the week, Dancin' Joe's wasn't nearly as crowded as he remembered. Braced with a beer or two, he chanced the dance floor with Georgina. She *did* know how to dance. She also knew how to teach. Before he knew it, he had forgotten he had two left feet, and he was following her directions determinedly.

And no one bothered him. In fact, by the time they were into his lesson, several more patrons had joined in, and Georgina was conducting a class on country dancing. Everyone was loving it. She was hysterically funny, had the patience of a saint, and had a charming and sneaky way of instilling self-esteem into the most negative of characters.

The crowd loved her. In her jeans, plaid shirt, and sneakers, she looked a little like a country-style cheerleader. She even had the band in the palm of her hand, making them stop and repeat and start again, as her avid learners conquered each section of the dance.

When they took a break, George headed to the ladies' room. On her way back, a youngish man stopped her in the dark corridor. "Hey, honey, how about you and me blowing this joint, and going for a ride in my pickup truck?"

"I don't think so, dear, but thanks for the offer."

"I can promise you a more exciting time than you'll have here, baby."

Her eyes softened. "Well, maybe . . . but I'm still declining. I'm kinda . . . involved."

He grunted and moved away.

By the end of the evening, Rockford could confidently do the steps to three songs, and felt an inordinate sense of accomplishment.

"Feels even better than passing the bar, eh cowboy?" Georgina joked. The funny thing was, it was true.

George was always surprising him. That was almost a lifelong thing. Even as a tiny child, she had been one to question and to attack problems that others would rather avoid. She was never afraid of risk, and had driven their parents crazy with her inability (or unwillingness) to accept the social rules of the wealthy world she lived in. At the age of five, she had practically created a riot at the Harrison mansion. In the midst of a formal ball being given in honor of the governor, she had made a dramatic entrance by dancing like a tightrope walker on the well-polished bannister of the grand stairway.

When their father had bellowed his disapproval, she had put her hands on her hips, standing on the newel post at the end of the bannister, and facing him squarely. "I just wanted to be taller," she had stated with dignity, before turning and gracefully walking back *up* the bannister, without even a wobble. The society pages had had fun with that one. Their mother had had palpitations.

Everyone had been amazed when Georgina Harrison had entered the convent, but in truth, their parents had probably been relieved. She could just as well have been an international terrorist, fighting for the rights of the oppressed! But seriously, he had come to understand and respect his tiny but impressive sibling in her fight for mankind.

As they drove back into town, he thanked her, both for the dance lesson, and for the wisdom of keeping him busy on this night of disappointment and pain. She smiled gently at her giant big brother. "It'll work out with Willow, you'll see."

And she meant it. She'd come up with a plan. . . .

Rockford had been immediately recognized when he had appeared at Dancin' Joe's.

"The uncoordinated cowboy is back, sir," a man reported to Charley Morse at his back table.

"With the blond realtor?"

"No, sir. He's with a small woman, dark hair. Not as much of a looker as the blond, but with enough energy to power an entire town. She's giving dance lessons."

"The blond dumped him, I bet. She's a sassy thing. Had car trouble, I hear."

The first man smirked. "That's what I hear. Hope it don't rain tonight."

"Is he driving the same bomb as before?"

"The same."

"Well, he's probably nothing to worry about, but keep an eye out. Let me know if there's any problems."

"Yeah, well, I'm gonna go get a free dance lesson."

"You need it." Charley Morse had laughed.

But he had had people keep an eye on the cowboy and

the dance teacher, because he was nervous about this whole deal. And he didn't like being nervous, especially when there was so much at stake.

But they hadn't bothered anybody, and finally they had left, which should have helped the nervousness Charley Morse felt. But it didn't. He was still nervous, and the deal still stunk. He couldn't wait to accomplish what he had been told to do, to get it over with. He didn't like problems.

So he'd better check out the cowboy, one way or another. He wrote a note on a piece of paper, and motioned to one of his men, who came quickly.

"Call St. Francis Parish, and leave this message for that nun, Sister George."

The man dutifully disappeared, and went to make his call from the office.

"Let me find out why there's a nun who lets a cowboy drive around a car she rented. I gotta find out who that joker is. Then I'll decide what to do about him."

Willow had been at home, and had heard the phone ring when Rockford had called. She had known that he would call. She had also known that emotionally she couldn't afford to talk to him.

But she had smiled when she had heard his message. A lawyer, that's for sure. And he had made his case. She had sat and thought about his words, replaying them many times as she thought, loving the timbre of his voice.

Was there a simple explanation? Had she jumped to conclusions? Or would he just try to convince her of that, knowing that there was another woman in the picture? Could she trust him? Trust. It burned like a hot poker in her heart.

She thought of his face. An honorable face. A strong face. She should listen. She *would* listen. She could almost feel his hands on her face, his lips . . . she wanted to trust, to believe. Could she?

By the time she got the courage to call him, there was no answer. It felt like a fist had tightened over her heart. *Rockford, where are you?*

"I'm not here right now, please leave a message." She waited for the beep. "This is Willow, counselor. Call me to schedule a hearing. Never let it be said that I didn't believe in the American way. I'll listen."

She curled up on the couch after hanging up the phone, pulling a comforter over her. She was exhausted. It had been a day of highs and lows, and it had taken its toll. The feelings came charging at her, as soon as she got still. She couldn't believe it, but she couldn't stop it. Before she knew it, Wilhemina Blake began to cry. She sobbed and sobbed, curled up in a ball, and clutched the comforter tightly to her, as if it was a security blanket. And in a way, it was. Finally, unbelievably, the tears ceased, just as they had begun, and Willow fell asleep.

Chapter Fourteen

Willow felt groggy when she arrived at the office the next morning. She had driven the Miata to be repaired, and had gotten a ride to work from one of the repairmen. He promised to deliver the car by noon.

Whenever she greeted a day feeling tired and low, she always chose flamboyant clothes to perk up her mood. Today was a good example. The polished cotton material of her fitted waist jacket boasted a brilliant print of bright pink and green flowers. A pleated miniskirt of matching pink left her long legs exposed. Her stockings were hot pink. So were her shoes.

Coming in the door, she looked like a flash of color, a rainbow streak of brightness.

Mildred sat at her desk by the wall, and gave a shy smile.

"Looking bright today, Willow. But the face doesn't match. Is everything okay?"

Willow laughed. "I can tell you know me, Mildred. I'm pushing the worries away."

Mildred nodded, understanding. She felt she was the extreme opposite of Willow in style, sitting in her prim gray cotton shirtwaist dress with its white Peter Pan collar. But she could see and identify with the myriad of emotions her coworker displayed, and she both respected her, and held her in awe.

She appreciated Willow's courage, her forthright way of stating her case and making her opinion known. She loved the creativity and daring she showed in her dress and sales style, and many times had wished she could do the same.

She also sensed the scars that Willow had from her past, and identified with those, too. They had never really talked about their childhoods; they had never socialized beyond their jobs. But there was a bond there, and Mildred cherished it.

"Anything I can do to help, just let me know."

Willow smiled. "Thanks! Let's see what today brings."

But there wasn't time for conversation after that, because the phones started ringing, Gail arrived, and Reynolds Realty was in full swing.

The call from the police came in late morning. The Harris farmhouse had been broken into and vandalized. The floorboards on the first floor had all been ripped up. Police had no clues. They were still looking for Charley Morse for questioning.

Sister George was worried. She sat in her small office at the back of the rectory, chewing her thumbnail, and wondering what to do. The telephone message she had received was sitting before her on the much used teacher's desk that the pastor had confiscated for her when she had arrived to handle the parish social needs several years before.

It wasn't the message itself that had her worried. Georgina got similar messages every day of the week. "Sister George, please return this call. The man wants to talk to you confidentially about a family problem."

Confidential family problems were her job. Messages could mean a difficult divorce, or an addiction problem. It could be a difficult relative, decisions about the elderly, financial crisis, abuse. She had heard it all before.

So she had dialed the number, speaking with "Joe," as instructed. And Joe had been very elusive. He wouldn't say a word about the problem on the phone. He had wanted her to meet with him, and she had accepted. The meeting had been set for early afternoon, at a small sandwich shop in town.

The situation wasn't extremely unusual, but a few small things had upset her unerring sense of radar. There had been country music in the background. Joe was calling from a public place, yet he had answered the phone himself. He had just not seemed to her like a man who was truly concerned about one of the human crises that would lead one to seek help from the church. To be honest, he didn't seem like a Joe at all. An assumed name? A phony problem? Why would anyone want to meet with a nun under false pretense? But these were small concerns, and not enough to cause true doubt.

It was her ears that got her into trouble. At the end of the conversation, while she was writing the time and location in her small diary, her ears had picked up on the background noise on the phone line, and what she had heard had made her stomach roll.

Through the faint sound of country music, and the occasional clink of glasses, the words of a background voice reverberated in her ear. "... Slergetti's order," the distant voice had said to someone. But then "Joe" had confirmed the meeting time, and had hung up the phone, leaving her sitting in dismay and shock.

Her first thought was that the call had come from Dancin' Joe's. Somehow, this call was related to the Charley Morse thing that Rockford and Willow had gotten involved in. Rockford and Willow. She thought of Peter, his violent death, his funeral. And his unpunished killer. Marco Slergetti.

What had Willow and Rockford stumbled into? She was absolutely sure that her headstrong brother had no glimmer of suspicion that his life was entwined again with Slergetti's in any way. She was also absolutely sure what he would do when he found out. No amount of logic or reason or restraint would hold him back. He would go after the mobster with every ounce of energy he could muster. And Rockford might end up dead. Like Peter.

Her small hands, usually so calm and competent, were shaking violently. She crumpled the message into a ball, and stuffed it into her pocket. Slergetti in Pennsylvania? There was only one tie that she could think of, and that was Rockford Farquahar Harrision III. He was after her brother. She swallowed hard. She needed help. The police? Probably, but not yet. First, she needed to talk to the only person she knew of who had the strength to keep her brother from getting killed. She went to find Willow.

George arrived at Willow's office just as the repaired car was being delivered. "Thanks, Benny!" she hollered as he pulled away, patting her Miata lovingly. "You look good, car!"

"Back to normal, Willow?" George asked.

"Don't know the meaning of the word, Sister. How are you today? Any problems with the home? I hear the fund is going well."

"It's great, Willow, but that's not why I'm here. I need to talk to you about something . . . important. Really important."

Willow froze as she looked into the small nun's face. She had never seen her look so serious, so scared.

"Come into the office, George. We'll talk."

She led her into the back room, asking Mildred to hold all her calls.

"It's about Rockford," the little nun began, her voice quaking. "I have a terrible fear that he's in trouble."

"I got a phone call today, Willow." She explained about the phone call, and her suspicions that it was tied into Dancin' Joe's and Marco Slergetti and Rockford.

"But what could you possibly have to do with Dancin' Joe's, Sister? I don't understand."

"We went there, Rockford and I, when I came home and found him last night. Maybe someone recognized me, and wants to use me to get to him." She hung her head. "I just don't know. I only know I'm afraid."

"You went to Dancin' Joe's with Rockford Harrison?" Willow's eyes were round with surprise. "When you came *home* and found him? You *live* with Rockford?" It was incredible. A nun.

But George laughed. "Ah, yes, I almost forgot we hadn't straightened that part out. It was *my* underwear in the bathroom."

It took a lot to shock Willow Blake. She was shocked.

"But you're a nun! He lives with a sister?"

Now George laughed out loud. "Yes, I guess you could say that. Now shut your mouth; you rather resemble a fish. Talk about thinking the worst of people! Yes, I'm a sister. I'm *his* sister. Formerly Miss Georgina Harrison, now Sister George. Nice to meet you." She stuck out her hand.

Willow plopped into a chair, letting out all her breath. "Boy, George, I have a great imagination, but I wouldn't have thought that one up in all the world."

"Well, getting back to what's more important than whose's underwear is whose, I'm really scared to death. You see, I was supposed to meet with Joe at Midway Diner at 4:00 P.M. today. But while I was writing that down, I heard voices in the background say 'Slergetti's orders.' That's what the voice said. Marco Slergetti. The disgusting mobster that has been able to escape capture all this time. Peter's killer. And now he's after Rockford."

Willow felt herself pale. She knew, too, what the information would do to Rockford. She felt a flash of fear for the Burdetts, if such a ruthless man were involved in their disappearance. She swallowed hard.

"We have to tell the police, George. You simply can't meet this guy. If it's a trap to get to Rockford, you have to avoid it. We need help here."

The little nun nodded. "I'll do anything to protect my brother, Willow."

"I'll call the detective, George. Just sit tight. And keep an eye on Rockford. Just promise me you won't go near that diner."

"Okay. I'm supposed to go to a meeting for the senior citizens in the parish," she said softly, as Willow walked her to the door. "It's so strange to do something so normal when there's so much at stake."

"That's how life is, isn't it?" Suddenly she had an idea. "But we can jazz up normal just a bit." She took the keys to the gray rental out of George's hands, exchanging them for the keys she had fished out of her pocket. "Take the Miata. Put the top down. Take the seniors for a ride!"

George laughed. "I'm not sure about that—think about their hairdos . . . but maybe. Would it be all right?"

"Go for it, crazy lady." She reached in and put down the hood of the car.

George climbed in excitedly. "Now this is really cool."

"Goes right with you, Georgina Harrison. Have fun. And don't worry too much."

Georgina pulled away from the curb with a squeal of the tires. "Thanks," she yelled, waving over her head as she moved down the street.

Willow stood watching her, worrying enough for the both of them. She spun on her heel and went back into the office to call the police.

Chapter Fifteen

Detective Dunn was out of the office. Willow left him a message, asking him to call as soon as he could. Her second call was to Rockford, who she found out was closeted in a meeting. She left him a message, too.

The afternoon dragged by, with Willow doing her never-ending paperwork, and talking to real estate clients on the telephone. There was no word from the detective or Rockford, and by 3:30, Willow's nerves were stretched taut.

The unknown voice on the phone would be waiting at the sandwich shop at 4:00 P.M. He was an important, dangerous link to Rockford's past. The opportunity to find out more would be lost, because Willow hadn't been able to share the information she had heard with the police so that they could investigate.

A few more long minutes ticked by in the office, silent now except for Mildred's soft voice describing property on the phone. A plan hatched in Willow's mind, and her adrenaline began to flow.

"Mildred," she said quietly, when her coworker hung up the receiver from her latest call, "I need you to help me with something. It's a bit of a weird request."

Mildred smiled uncertainly. Willow's requests were practically world renowned. But she listened to the plan, reacting with shock and disbelief, then with a certain kind of respect, as she heard the details.

"I don't know, Willow, it sounds dangerous. Shouldn't you just wait for the police?"

"I tried that. Detective Dunn didn't call back. But if he does, you have my permission to fill him in. I just can't let this opportunity go by."

Mildred shook her head. "I'll look so . . . different. I'm not sure it's a good idea."

"It'll be fine. Come on, help me out."

They put the phone lines on hold for a few minutes, and a most amazing transformation took place. In a flash, Mildred Mansfield became a flash of flowers and color, dressed in Willow's flamboyant short-skirted suit, pink stockings and all. Her embarrassed cheeks had turned pink, to match.

"Pretty cool, Mildred. What a change! I swear, you look ten years younger!"

"You look a bit different yourself, Willow Blake. I hope we're not going to regret this. I don't think even you can pull this off. You're not exactly the type to be a nun."

Willow laughed out loud and looked at herself one last time in the mirror. The gray dress with the little round collar was belted in white at the waist. It hung demurely below her knees. Mildred's no-nonsense shoes had taken the place of the pink heels. A simple gold cross hung at her neck. On her head, she wore a large cloth napkin, folded diagonally like a scarf, and anchored behind her neck.

"Just call me Sister, please. I hope this isn't some kind of a sin, impersonating a nun. It's for a good cause."

Mildred sighed. "Just go and get it over with, Willow. If the police call, I'll send the detective over. Meanwhile, just be careful. And when you're done, you can get rid of that dress." She shuddered. "I had no idea I looked like that."

She smoothed the flowered skirt over her thighs.

"Well, you look pretty good now, Millie! The suit's yours. And when this is over, maybe we can go shopping together!"

Mildred laughed. "If I start dressing like this, Mr. Reynolds won't know what has gotten into me when he comes back."

"You're great, Millie. Thanks a lot for helping me out." Mildred's flushed face smiled.

There were a handful of cars in the lot at the sandwich shop. Willow parked the gray rental in an open spot and went inside, sitting quickly at a booth by the door and looking around expectantly. A waitress approached, and she ordered a cup of coffee. She sipped it slowly. In a few minutes, a man stood up from a stool at the counter and headed her way. She swallowed hard as he slipped into the booth across from her.

" 'Afternoon, Sister," he said in a deep voice. "I'm Joe. Thanks for coming."

She nodded, at first not trusting her voice.

"I got a problem with my brother," he began, launching into a long speech about a troubled man with a penchant for drink and gambling that was taking its toll on the family.

Willow listened, dismay replacing the fear that she had felt when she arrived. The poor man was pouring his heart out to her, and she was a fraud. She swallowed hard.

"Sounds like he's got his share of problems. Probably needs more help than you or I could give him. Have you spoken to a doctor about him? Gotten him any psychological support?"

Gee, she sounded like Dear Abby.

"Is that what I should do, Sister? Try to get some professional help for him? How about if I talk to a priest?"

"Good idea. Good idea." She'd relay the information to

George, so at least the man wouldn't be totally wasting his time. Guilt was a mighty powerful emotion.

"I'll do that." The man made a move to get up. "By the way, Sister, that's a nice car you're driving. Have it long?" His eyes narrowed a bit at the question, and Willow's guilt started to ebb away.

"Not too long. Why?"

"Just wondered. I thought I saw it somewhere before. Maybe not." She could feel his eyes assessing her, trying to read her reaction.

Her mind was alert now. The guilt had dissipated, and she smelled danger. George had been contacted because of the car. Her instincts, and her fears, were right. And if Marco Slergetti were involved, and he discovered that George was Rockford's sister, she would be in big trouble.

"Ah well, the car gets around. Lots of people borrow it. I drive it occasionally, but so do many other people. I guess you could have seen it anywhere."

He seemed satisfied. She couldn't believe it, but he actually accepted her as a nun.

She decided to change the subject. "So where do you work? It sounded like a noisy place when you called. Country music in the background."

His eyes narrowed again. "Nowhere special. Just a restaurant." He shifted in his seat, not comfortable at being on the receiving end of a question.

"Well, okay, Sister. I'll think about getting some more help for my brother. I guess I've taken enough of your time."

He had scrambled to his feet, wasting no time in getting out the door. Willow followed thoughtfully, watching him pull away in an old Volkswagen.

Willow returned to a frantic office. Along with the normally busy real estate business, the phones had been ringing off the wall. Rockford had been calling nonstop, looking for her. George had called several times. But also, she had received several phone calls from people who were inquiring about donating to the new AIDS Fund that they had read about in the newspaper.

Gail was busily manning the telephone, raising one eyebrow as she surveyed Willow's sedate religious outfit. When there was a break in the line of calls, she turned to Willow with a grin. "I'm not sure what's going on in this place, with you looking a little like Mother Theresa, and Mildred looking like a fashion queen, but as long as you answer these phone calls, I'm asking no questions!" She pushed a stack of messages toward Willow. "Mildred is out showing property with a banker who is relocating to this area. He couldn't keep his eyes off her in those hot pink stockings. It's a sure deal if I ever saw one!"

"How about these donation calls? What's the story on them?" Gail handed her the daily newspaper.

"Check out the story on page three. You've done it, Willow. With a little help from that nun you've met, you're going to get the help you need for the AIDS house."

Willow landed at her desk, opening the paper with a snap. A picture of George . . . Sister George, for once wearing her habit, graced the page in front of her. *AIDS Home Trust Fund established by anonymous donor to assist local residents.*

George's bubbly exuberance had been captured in the article, applauding the giant step that had been taken toward progress, and soliciting further contributions from the paper's readership. Willow's name and number were listed to call for information. Smiling, she folded the paper and put it on the corner of her desk. That was good news in an otherwise bleak day.

She turned her attention to answering her phone messages.

* * *

"You're an imbecile." The man's low voice was hushed, deadly. The young man standing before him swallowed hard, bile rising in his throat, the taste of fear.

He looked down at the folded newspaper that had been tossed at him. "It was a mistake, sir. Anybody could have made it."

"I don't pay people to make mistakes. I don't allow people to make mistakes."

"But she was a nun. She was dressed like a nun."

A fierce hand banged down on the newspaper. "This is the nun. This is Sister George from St. Francis's. Whoever you met with is an imposter, you idiot. You were tricked."

Eyes down, the man swallowed hard, sweat rolling like a river down his back.

"Get me what I need," the voice continued, low and mean. "Last chance. No more mistakes. Go."

The dismissal was curt, to the point. He didn't waste any time removing himself.

Willow's first call was to Rockford. While apologizing wasn't high on her list of things she loved to do, she knew when it was warranted.

"I'm sorry I got upset the other night. I've met your sister . . . the sister. You know what I mean. I jumped to conclusions that you were involved with somebody. . . ."

"I'm to blame too, Willow. I should have explained about living with Georgina. It's just that when George is involved, the situation is a little . . . complicated, so I put it off."

"Well, I'm glad that's behind us. I like to be open and up-front. . . ."

As she said the words, a tightness was growing in her stomach. Open? Up-front? After hearing Georgina and her fear of Marco Slergetti, and what his appearance could do to Rockford's feelings of guilt and anger, the last thing she was going to do was to be open and up-front about her fears until she had figured out what was going on.

"I'll pick you up in a little bit and we'll talk things out, all right?"

She agreed, running her fingers lightly over her lips, and remembering the taste and feel of him. Answers. She'd find answers and be free to explore this new and burning desire to be with this complicated man without keeping secrets from him.

Her next call was to Georgina. "Sister George, you look great in the newspaper. I'm so excited about the trust. Who's the anonymous donor?"

"Top secret. I promised. We can do a lot with that money, and more contributions are pouring in. But enough of that . . . any more news about you-know-who? I haven't heard anything new."

Had she deterred the man she had met from worrying about Georgina? She certainly hoped so. She decided to tell Georgina what she had done.

"You went and met the man?" the little nun screeched. "Dressed as a nun?"

There was a long pause, while Willow waited for her reaction. It wasn't what she expected. Georgina began to giggle.

"Oh, man, I wish I could have seen that. I wish the bishop could have seen that. I wish Rockford could have."

"I didn't do it for entertainment, George," she said, trying to keep the smile out of her voice. "I wanted to see what the man was after, why he had called you. It was because of the car. They must have traced the car when we took it to Dancin' Joe's. I told him it was driven by a lot of people. He seemed to accept that."

Georgina sobered up. "We have to tell Rockford."

Willow knew it was true. "He's coming here in a little while. Want to join us?" Georgina agreed.

She plowed her way through the rest of her phone messages, a feeling of anticipation growing at the thought of seeing Rockford, and pushing away the growing feelings of fear and apprehension about Charley Morse and Marco Slergetti.

Chapter Sixteen

Rockford walked in the door of the real estate office just as Willow received a phone call. His mind registered delight at seeing her, curiosity at the uncharacteristic look of her dress, and surprise at seeing his sister Georgina gracing the chair by her desk.

But as he crossed the room toward her, a bell of alarm rang in his head. From a few short words on the telephone, he could feel, as well as see, Willow's tense reaction to the call. Her expressive face froze, then displayed a kaleidoscope of emotions as she listened to the phone: anger, dismay, then fear.

She raised her face to meet his eyes, as she deposited the phone receiver onto its cradle. He saw the pain there in her eyes, and felt the power of her need. He automatically lifted her from her chair, pulling her into his strong arms.

"What is it? What's happened?"

Her face was pale as she struggled to plant her feet firmly, shaking her head, trying to compose herself.

"Oh, Rockford. That was the police. It's about the Burdett farm. There's been a terrible fire at the farmhouse. The fire company has just managed to put it out." Her voice caught in a sob.

"It's okay, Willow," he said softly, running his hand up and down her back. "It's just a building. The Burdetts weren't there."

"But that's just it!" she wailed, her fingers digging into his arms. "When they got the fire under control, and they began to sift through the wreckage, they found . . . two bodies. . . ."

He pulled her close again, and she nestled her head into his neck. "It's my fault, Rockford, it's my fault. If I had gone back to the farm that first night, maybe this wouldn't have happened. . . ."

He swallowed hard, not knowing what to say, but desperately wanting to help her. His eyes met George's, perched on the chair across from the desk. *"Go ahead,"* her expressive eyes pleaded. *"Follow your instincts."* His sister's quiet confidence gave him courage.

"You are not to blame for whatever has happened at that farm, Wilhemina Blake. You are strong and trustworthy and caring, and you did the best you could. No one could have done more." His words were soft and comforting, and she found herself clinging to them in her pain.

A few silent minutes passed, until her breath became more even. She stood straight again, and looked into his eyes.

"Well, I couldn't stop it from happening, maybe, but I'm not going to stop until I find out who's to blame." She straightened her thin shoulders defiantly.

"I was afraid you were going to say that. I *knew* you were going to say that."

"I have to go out to the farm. I have to . . . see. Will you come?"

There was no way he was going to let her go on her own, and no way, he knew absolutely, that he could stop her. "Sure, I'll come."

Georgina stood quickly to her feet. "I'm going to leave this development to you two, and get back to the parish for now. We'll handle our other . . . business later, all right, Willow?"

The news about Marco Slergetti would wait until she had the information about the Burdetts.

George punched her brother in the arm on her way out the door. "Take care of her. Don't mess things up."

"Spoken like a person who believes in me."

"Spoken like a person who *knows* you!" With a quick smile, Georgina was gone.

"I didn't know she was your sister. You didn't tell me."

"It's not something I brag about." He laughed gently. "She has a rather persuasive quality." He looked suddenly down at Willow's plain gray dress and cross. Alarm crossed his face.

"Oh no, you look like a nun . . . she didn't persuade you—"

Despite the heaviness of her heart, Willow laughed. "Just a costume, counselor. I'll tell you about it later. Come on, let's face this farmhouse."

George had left in the gray car, so they took the Miata to the Burdett farm. Rumbling down the long stony driveway, Willow thought of the little farm couple with sadness. The air smelled dank and smoky, and a darkness, like a dusty cloud, hovered over the place.

The barn could be seen through the veil of smoke as they pulled in. The place where the house had been was nothing more than a charred black skeleton jutting up into the sky. Part of the porch room remained, a sad reminder of what had been. In the flower beds by the door, Willow could see the blossoms that had shortly before been bursting with life now shriveled and dried from the excessive heat. She felt a lump in her throat.

There was one fire truck remaining, as a precaution against any sudden recombustion at the fire site. Wisps of smoke still meandered upward from somewhere within the rubble. Along the driveway, the grass had turned to mud from the fire hoses and black-booted feet of the firemen.

Two police cars and a black van were parked by the door. Officers and investigators were already climbing through the blackened beams.

When they stepped from the car, Detective Dunn came to greet them.

"Terrible thing, fire," he said, clearing his throat as he approached. "Not much doubt it was arson."

"But why, why?" Willow said softly.

"It's going to take some figuring to get the lowdown on this one, Miss Blake. It's a strange thing . . . preliminary investigation seems to indicate that the floorboards were all torn up on the first floor before the fire was started, for some strange reason. Nails were found piled in one spot, remains of boards in another. Any ideas about that?"

"Why would somebody tear up the floorboards? This is awful." She swallowed hard. "Where did you find the Burdetts?"

The detective squinted and looked at her strangely. "Bodies were found in the basement. Looks like they were shot in the back of the head, execution style."

Willow felt her eyes swimming with tears. Rockford tightened his arm around her, and she absorbed his strength.

Her voice was hoarse when she spoke. "You've got to find that Charley Morse. He's a part of this. You've got to find him."

The detective shook his head. "No ma'am, I don't have to find him. I already found him, but he doesn't have any answers. You've got it all wrong."

"What are you talking about?"

"The bodies in the basement . . . they're not the Burdetts. One is Charley Morse, and another is a local man named Joe Johnson."

Willow swallowed hard.

Charley Morse and the man from the diner? She thought she was going to be sick.

"But where are the Burdetts?" She cried in frustration.

"That's what I want to know, young lady," the now stern-faced detective replied. "They've disappeared from their house, supposedly with half a million dollars. Then the place is burned down, and two bodies were found. This changes everything. We've put out another APB for them, only this time it's for suspicion of murder."

For the first time in her life, Willow Blake was speechless.

Chapter Seventeen

They had returned to Willow's cottage, still reeling from the news. Willow was seething with indignation. Suspicion of murder? The Burdetts?

Rockford just shook his head. "Give it time, Willow. They'll figure this thing out."

"Right," snarled Willow. "We're seeing firsthand how efficient and clever those police are. We have to have a plan."

"The only plan I have right now is to kiss you." He pulled her quickly into his arms, covering her mouth with his.

She drew in her breath harshly, her body stiffening as his lips touched hers. But she didn't pull away. She couldn't.

She could feel something like an electric current passing through her, leaving her feeling weak and wobbly-legged. Still stiff, she leaned against him, trying to understand the war that was raging inside of her.

He felt so good. His strong arms were wrapped securely around her, not binding her, but leaving no doubt about his feelings. His mouth was gentle upon hers, but insistent. It felt so right, so safe.

And yet, voices in her head were screaming at her to pull away, to come to her senses, to reinforce the emotional barriers that had come to be so second nature to her. She didn't trust men. She didn't want to trust men. And yet . . .

His kiss worked its magic upon her, and she melted from its heat. Slowly, the tenseness left her body, replaced by a feeling of floating as he ran his hands gently up and down her back. Slowly, her lips began to quiver, as the negative messages in her mind began to recede. She kissed him back and he responded.

But he knew this woman, and she had somehow touched his heart with her untrusting vulnerability, and her outrageous moral courage. If he followed his instincts, it would be the end, instead of the beginning. When she suddenly pulled back, he let her go with a smile.

It wasn't going to be enough to just put out the fire that raged in him. This was more. She was more. And while that new and amazing realization flowed over him, enabling him to conquer his impatience, he instinctively knew that he would wait until Willow was ready.

His breath was coming hard, and his voice was shaky as he pulled his head back to look into her eyes.

"Someday, Willow. Someday. We belong together."

She was exhausted suddenly, from the wide range of emotions that had run rampant through the day.

She nestled up next to him as they sat down on the couch, tucking herself tightly against him, and they both fell asleep.

Chapter Eighteen

Rockford was the first to open his eyes a few hours later. The sun had disappeared with the early evening, leaving the sky outside the window a smoky gray as night descended. He didn't move, wanting to savor the warm feeling of Willow snuggled up next to him, tucked gently against his body as she slept. The fit was so right. It felt so good. He savored the moment.

The appealing smell of her perfume still lingered in his nostrils, reminding him of the tender moments he had had with her. But through the open windows of her cottage, another smell permeated the air . . . the remains of the pungent smell of fire, smoke, and sodden ash from the Burdett farm down the road. The apprehensions he had felt during the long day returned full force. The fire had been the last in a series of unsettling events. His mind felt a little scrambled, like pieces of a giant jigsaw puzzle floating around. Facts and information vital to providing answers were resisting coming together in any semblance of order.

Willow had been right from the start. Something was definitely going on in Ryerstown. Her concerns about Charley Morse had been justifiable, but limited in scope. Because Charley Morse had been expendable, inconsequential, when all was said and done. He had been simply one piece in the dangerous jigsaw puzzle. But what about Willow? Was she another piece, by her involvement in the real estate deal? Was Willow in danger? Fear burned like acid in his stomach. Visions of Peter, blood spilling, stormed through his mind, torturing him.

Quietly, careful not to disturb her sleeping form, he rose from the couch. He looked down at her face, still relaxed in sleep. She was going to be mad when she woke up. She'd be way past furious that he was gone. But keeping her alive was important enough to risk it. She would never stop her headstrong investigation into the Burdetts' disappearance, and every step she took could be drawing her closer to tragedy, unless he found the answers first. He wasn't going to lose her now. He sneaked out of the room, out of the cottage, heading for town, as the last light of day dimmed to night. You had to move pretty quickly to keep even one step ahead of Wilhemina Blake.

Willow awakened to the rumble of the car engine as Rockford pulled out of the driveway. Instantly alert, her arm searched the couch where he had been. Rockford was gone. Straining to look out the window, she could see the red twinkle of his taillights in the distance.

Feelings rushed through her like a freight train out of control. Rockford had slinked away in the darkness of night, leaving her without a word. She felt doubt. They had been so close . . . she felt so vulnerable. Had she meant so little to him?

But then she began to worry. Had something gone wrong? Had something else happened? She could still smell the lingering odor of wet ash that hovered in the air. She thought of the Burdetts, of Charley Morse.

Or had Rockford taken off to find new answers, to investigate an idea that had occurred to him in the unconsciousness of sleep? He'd taken off without her, either to avoid her or to protect her. The minute she thought it, she knew it was true. The worry turned to rage.

Willow bounded from the couch, slipping her feet into

sneakers. By the time mere seconds had passed, her long legs had carried her out the door, and her Miata was roaring toward town. She'd find him. She'd find out what he was up to, and she'd tell him what she felt about being left behind.

Rockford knew of only one place to start seeking answers. The real estate deal had been presented with Porter as lawyer, holding power of attorney. However deeply Porter had been involved with Charley Morse, it had included trust to handle the paperwork for purchasing two properties to the tune of half a million each. That was deep enough for Rockford. Porter had better come up with some answers.

He arrived at his office building, finding a parking space easily, as businesses and offices closed early in Ryerstown. The legal office building was dark. He let himself in through the heavy wooden doors with his own key, and silently moved toward his office without turning on a light.

He felt a bit like a culprit sneaking around in the dark, but he couldn't erase the apprehension and worry that nagged at him. He closed the door of his office and turned on his office light. The room sprang to life, taking away the shadows. It was normal, undisturbed. His apprehensions felt a little silly.

Sitting at his desk, he thumbed through his Rolodex and found Porter's home telephone number, and dialed it quickly.

"I'm not here to answer your call right now, but I'll call you back as soon as possible. Leave your name and number at the beep. . . ."

"Darn," Rockford said, ignoring the beep, banging one fist on the desk, and banging the phone back into the cradle with the other. "Where the heck is he?"

Maybe it was a general attack of paranoia, but he thought he had heard a trace of something in Porter's taped voice.

Not distress exactly, but something akin to it. There was a touch of nervousness. The self-assured, blustering attorney who had intimidated many a witness on the stand didn't sound quite as confident.

He thought for a moment, then got up from his desk. There was a lot at stake here . . . and he was going to have to violate some of his own code of ethics. Peter's voice lingered in his memory. *"It's the principle of the thing."*

He crossed the hall to Porter's office door. It was locked.

With only a flash of conscience, he strode in the darkness to Prudence's desk in the front hall. He turned on her desk lamp, and began opening her drawers. At the back of her bottom drawer, he found what he was looking for: the set of master office keys that she kept for his uncle. He flipped off the light, and was back at Porter's door within seconds. The first key on the ring fit the lock. The door swung open.

The room smelled slightly of pipe smoke, reminding him of Porter. The old-fashioned desk lamp cast a slightly orange glow when he pulled the chain. The desk before him was in disarray. Papers were scattered across its top. A file was open, its contents strewn across the top of the pile. It looked like Porter had left in a hurry. His pipe stood upside down in an ashtray, ashes long cold.

Rockford sat at the desk, his hands rapidly going through the papers on the desk. He felt a fist close around his heart. The open file was what he dreaded—the real estate papers from the Burdett farm sale. Willow's name leaped up at him from a handwritten note from Prudence on the top of the file. *Call Willow Blake, office 555-3413 or home 555-1678.* It was dated the day the real estate transaction had begun.

He put the file back together, then tacked the other paper on the desk. He found a small pile of phone messages taken by Prudence. He read the first. *See me as soon as you come in.* It was a command appearance from his uncle.

Call me about this New York business right away, the next message said. Then, *Call me now!* On both, the return number was familiar to him. It was his old law firm. Seeing the extension number made the hair on the back of his neck tingle. It was his father's law office. His father had been trying to get in touch with Porter. Why?

He glanced around the room, trying to decide what to do next. His eye was caught by a small blinking red light in the corner of the dark room. He walked to it. A simple black telephone sat on the windowsill, attached to an answering machine. Porter had evidently installed a private line, unconnected to the office telephone system. There were two messages on the machine. He pushed the PLAY button with a strange sense of foreboding. "This is Morse, Big Shot," a gravelly, angry voice rang out. "You get in touch with me, or it'll be the last thing you do. . . ."

He had never talked to Charley Morse, but he had heard Willow's description of his conversations. He didn't know if Porter had ever gotten the message. But now it was too late. Making the phone call may have been one of the last things Charley Morse did. He shook his head as the message ended with a beep and the next one began.

"Call at eight tonight. 555-1099. No excuses." The voice was low and steady, not the excitable angry voice of Morse. The caller left no name, but it didn't matter. Rockford felt as if he had been punched in the gut by a prizefighter.

He knew the voice. He hated the voice. He had heard the voice almost daily for the better part of a year. He had listened to the slimy, cruel voice with his emotions intact. He had counseled him, he had defended him. He had helped him go free. And the voice had repaid him by sending a cold-blooded killer after his best friend. It was the voice of Marco Slergetti.

Bile rose in his throat as his head began to swim. Slergetti was not only back in the country, he was close by. The line had been clear and loud. The phone number hadn't included an area code. He was instantly horrified at the feelings of anger and revenge that exploded in him. He couldn't believe what he wanted to do to the owner of the voice. He swallowed hard.

The next thoughts that came traipsing through his mind had to do with fear. He knew the character of the man who was Marco Slergetti. He knew what he was capable of doing, he knew what he had done. And he knew that somehow, he was mixed up with Porter, and with Charley Morse, and therefore, unknowingly, with Willow Blake. His hands began to shake. He knew in that instant just how much he loved Willow. He would protect her with his life.

Automatically, he shut off the desk light, and walked quickly out of the office, back into his own. The clock read 8:00 P.M. The number from the phone message was etched indelibly on his mind. He knew what he had to do.

He sat at the desk and picked up the phone, dialing quickly. "Slergetti," the hated voice answered. "Who's this?" Rockford hung up the phone gently without saying a word. His heart was hammering inside. He wouldn't make the same mistake twice. Marco Slergetti was going to be behind bars, and this time, instead of getting him freed, he was going to get him caught. For Peter. For Willow. For himself. He needed to talk to the police. He rushed out the front door of the office, not looking left or right, forgetting, in his rush, the master keys he had stuffed into his pocket.

Willow watched him tear down the street. It hadn't been hard to find Rockford at his office; his desk lamp had shone like a beacon in the darkened building as she had pulled up the street. She had passed his car, parking about a block away, and had sneaked back to the office building soundlessly.

When she stepped up onto the front porch, she had been able to see right into his office, where he sat tensely at his desk. His face was drawn and angry, and she was amazed at the urge she had to rub his tense shoulders and ease his stress.

But her concern changed to confusion as she saw him pick up the phone, and dial a number from memory, punching the numbers into the phone pad with emotion. She stood in the darkness of the porch, watching through the window as his face contorted with rage. The phone hung up, he had strode from the office like a man on a mission, slamming the front door in his haste, and literally flew down the front steps and into his car.

He had passed only yards away, yet he hadn't see her standing in the shadows. Where was he going in such a hurry? What was he up to? She was torn. His car swerved down the street at a rapid pace, and hers was parked over a block away. She would lose him if she tried to follow.

But glancing at the front door, she saw the widened shadow where the heavy doors met. He had slammed the door in his haste, but hadn't checked it. It had bounced off the door post, and the lock hadn't caught. She pushed it gently with one hand, and it swung inward. The office was open. She shrugged her shoulders. She might not be able to catch up with him, but she might find out something about what he was up to! She slipped though the partly opened door, and closed it behind her. She was inside the law offices.

She felt her way to Rockford's office in the dark, not knowing she was repeating his actions. She found the desk, and turned on the light. The office looked undisturbed. She felt frustrated. He had left her behind. He had several minutes' head start from the cottage, and then he had several minutes while she had parked her car and had walked up the street. She didn't know what he had done in his office. She looked at the phone on his desk. She had seen him dial the phone. She picked up the receiver and hit the automatic redial button. A series of tones rang in her ear, then she could hear the phone ringing as the call went through. "Slergetti," a low voice said. She dropped the phone.

"Who's there?" The phone receiver lay on the desk, the squawking voice sounding distant, but there was no mistaking its agitation. "Who's got this number?" Then the click of a hangup, and the hum of the dial tone. Slowly, as if trying to move underwater, Willow hung up the phone.

Slergetti. Rockford Harrison had called Slergetti. While she and George had been foolishly concerned about letting Rockford know that Slergetti was around, worried about his rage, his anger over Peter's death . . . Willow swallowed hard, trying to compose herself, wanting to slow her racing heart. Why had he run to his office to call Slergetti? She had watched him punch the numbers into the phone. He hadn't even looked them up.

Her stomach was turning. Was Rockford involved with Slergetti? And if Slergetti had been involved with Charley Morse and the real estate deals, with the missing Burdetts, with Peter's death . . .

She hadn't realized that the tears were running down her face until they ran off her chin, making drops on the shiny desktop. Was she such a bad judge of character? Could she have been so wrong about Rockford? She thought of his hands caressing her, encouraging her, delighting her, only hours before. She thought of those same hands automatically pushing the buttons on the phone, connecting him to a mobster . . . an arsonist . . . a killer.

It seemed impossible. But she had seen it herself. She had redialed the number. She had heard Slergetti's voice.

She dried her tears, pushing away the feelings of loneliness and devastation that cut through her. It was going to be up to her to find out the truth . . . and to save the Burdetts if it wasn't already too late. She would trust no one in the process.

She left the office with a heavy heart, pulling the door shut tightly behind her. The lock clicked. She walked quickly to her car, mindful of the darkness of the empty street. She felt as if eyes were boring into her back, but even after glancing around, she saw no one. She pulled the Miata from the curb and headed home, her mind racing about the events of the day.

Chapter Nineteen

Rockford's mind was on automatic pilot as he drove the car at close to reckless speed. He crossed the river from Pennsylvania into New Jersey, moving rapidly northward toward New York. He was going home. He was going to see his father, while the rage was burning in his mind, while his heart was cold as stone.

Rockford had always looked up to his father. Rockford Farquahar Harrison II, the great and busy undisputed legal leader in the very competitive Manhattan arena. As a boy, he had also often longed for him, yearned for his attention, his time.

The elder Harrison had seen that his offspring had had everything that anyone could dream that they should—the best home, the best clothes, the best schools, the best staff. He was a man in control of a lot of money, and he shared with and provided for his family with pride and distinction. Except for his time. He hoarded his time for things he considered to be relevant and important priorities. He considered political events important. His legal duties were vital. His social contacts were kept strong.

But he hadn't found things like fishing, or sharing, or spending time with his young son or daughter to be worthy of a place on his To Do list. Yet, they had worshiped him from afar.

His mother was a dynamic, social woman. She ran the exclusive estate like a well-oiled machine. She sat on the board of many charities, raised funds for the needy, and made sure that her children's lives were comfortable and successful.

But Rockford had the strong suspicion that she had learned early on in her well-heeled marriage that love and easy companionship wouldn't be by-products of the union. He knew that his mother adored his father, and suspected that she would have been much happier with less materialism and more companionship. But she had adapted to the arrangement, and life had gone on.

Rockford had learned that the way to momentarily capture his father's attention was to succeed—to succeed in prep school, to excel in sports, to receive honors at college. He had done what was expected of him. He had finished his legal training, had passed the bar with flying colors, and had joined the firm as his father's son. Winning cases had been the next logical step in his quest to please his dad. He had also done that well. Until Peter. Until there was no Peter.

When he had lost his best friend, he had realized the void in his life. Peter had been his anchor, his confidant, his encourager, his conscience. His death had changed his life.

George had decided early on that she was not going to beg for emotional crumbs from the Harrison empire. She had left home, entered the convent, and pursued college in a habit. Always her own person, but never judging him for his choice to join his father's rat race, for a while he had seen her only at holidays when the family got together.

When he had moved away with George to Ryerstown, he had also moved away from the feeling that he had to perform to please his father. But he had never stopped loving his father. He had never stopped looking up to him. He had never once doubted, despite Peter's protests, his father's insistence that he personally handle the Slergetti case, and, as usual, win.

His father had seemed distraught at Peter's death, apologetic about the case after the fact. Except for his disappointment when Rockford had insisted on leaving the family firm, he had seemed comparatively caring and concerned.

Though he hadn't orchestrated the move to Pennsylvania, Rockford's father had accepted Georgina's meddling with the hopes of seeing his son come through his depression and lethargy.

And he had come through. He wasn't depressed and lethargic anymore. But he was enraged. He felt duped. He felt violated. Was his father involved with Marco Slergetti? Was the law firm intertwined with organized crime? Why had his revered father been calling Porter on his private line, a line also used by Marco Slergetti?

To feel that he had been set up to defend a vicious killer was bad enough . . . to have that fact backfire and cause Peter's death was too much to bear. But he would get answers tonight. He would challenge the father he had always looked up to and he would find out what part he had played, even inadvertently, in his best friend's death.

Because he wasn't going to risk tragedy a second time. Not with Willow. He was going to play out the scene until the last line tonight. He was going to bring Marco Slergetti to justice, even if he had to bring his father down in the process. There was danger in the air. He could feel it. And he wasn't going to let Willow Blake be burned by its flames, not while he had a breath left in his body.

By the time he had maneuvered the traffic and the beltways around the city, and had arrived at the familiar stone and wrought-iron gates that marked the entryway to the family estate, it was almost midnight. He punched in a code to open the electronic gate, took a deep breath, and drove the car down the long quiet drive.

It was a familiar ride, and yet it was new. He was a different person since the day he had left with Georgina. Maybe, he thought, finally he was a man.

He rounded the gracefully bended driveway, ready for the sight of the Harrison mansion to come into view. He expected to see its tasteful brass lampposts glowing, its windows lit with their welcoming golden haze.

The sight surprised him, though. Flashing, garish lights lit up the driveway in front of the main door. A large white vehicle was pulled up to the front door. In the steady flashes of light, Rockford read the side of the vehicle: AMBULANCE.

He leapt from his car, and tore across the front lawn, bounding up the entry steps, and almost colliding with the emergency technicians who were laboring to maneuver the stretcher bearing their patient. It was his father.

Chapter Twenty

Rockford could recognize him behind the oxygen mask. He could see that he was unconscious. There was an IV tube already inserted in his arm, a bag of clear fluid held high by an accompanying technician as they rushed through the door.

"Coming through . . . out of the way!" They passed him and slid the stretcher into the waiting ambulance without a second's delay.

"Wait! That's my father. What happened?" He grabbed the blue-overalled arm of a technician who was following the stretcher, carrying an extra oxygen tank. The man turned to him, compassion in his eyes, but clearly determined in his priorities.

"Sir, every second counts. Your father has had a major stroke. He'll be at Valley Memorial. His doctor has been alerted. Go help your mother, and follow us there. Now."

With a flash, the door of the ambulance slammed shut in front of his face, and the vehicle screeched into the night, lights flashing and sirens wailing.

It took a second for Rockford to orient himself. He was powerless. He had felt this way when Peter had died. It had amazed him then, and it amazed him now. Human beings liked to pretend that they had a semblance of control over their environment, power over their world.

But no one had power over death, not even his seemingly

141

omnipotent father. Was he dying? Acid burned in his stomach, and his head was banging like a jackhammer.

He leaped up the steps of the mansion that he had once called home, and went to find his mother.

She was sitting on an antique mahogany chair that sat in an alcove in the upstairs. Right beside the chair was a matching table, with a bouquet of flowers bursting with color. Funny, he thought, as the strangest little things registered on his mind, he had never seen anyone sit in that chair before. It had rested in its place of honor for all the years he could remember, decorating the upstairs hall.

His mother sat looking straight ahead, not moving at all. Her short, graying hair was perfectly coiffed, as usual. Her matronly dress was impeccable and classic. She could have been posing for a portrait as she sat in the quaint alcove, hands folded on her lap. But her eyes told the story. When he looked into her eyes, his throat constricted. Tears were flowing freely, literally pouring down her cheeks, as she stared straight ahead. He had never seen his mother cry, he realized. The sight almost broke his heart.

"Mother . . . Mom?" He dropped to his knees in front of her and pulled her forward so she rested her head on his shoulder. He could feel her welcome the embrace. She had always been so strong, so sure, so confident. But she looked beaten. He knew the feeling.

"Oh, Rockford, I'm so glad you're here." He held her gently, a million memories crowding his mind.

"Oh, Mom, I'm so sorry. What happened?"

She sniffed. "They think it's a stroke. He was on the phone. Something had upset him a lot, I think. He just fell over, dropping the phone. It was horrible."

His mind was racing, still not forgetting his original reasons for returning home. "Who was he talking to, Mom? Do you know?"

She shook her head.

"I just picked up the phone and called 911 and the ambulance came. I didn't know what to do. . . ."

"You did fine, Mom . . . just take it easy now."

She had dialed the phone, so there was no chance of automatically redialing the person his father had been talking to. But he was going to find out. Did that phone call cause the stroke? Would there be long-distance records? Mentally, he started making plans.

"Come on now, Mother. We need to get to the hospital."

He led her down the wide stairway, where Thomas, the longtime butler, stood wringing his hands in the entryway. For the first time since Rockford could remember, the stately and proper gentleman was lost for gracious words.

He put an arm around the black-suited shoulders. "I'll call you, Thomas, when we know something. I know this is hard. Can you hold things together here? It's important for Mother."

The elderly man straightened his shoulders. "Of course, sir . . . for Mrs. Harrison. I shall be on my toes." Being given the responsibility had restored his usual demeanor.

Rockford looked at him gratefully, and added, "I'm not sure what happened here, Thomas." He glanced quickly back up the stairs toward his father's private office and the telephone.

"I shall be the model of discretion, sir," the man said quietly under his breath, as he offered a sweater for Rockford's mother. "And I shall take specific note of phone calls."

Rockford grabbed the sweater for his mother, and helped her down the porch steps and into his car at the curb, giving an appreciative nod to Thomas for his insight.

Then they sped to the hospital, not knowing what they would find.

* * *

There are times when the senses can dredge up pleasant memories that bring happiness and good feelings in a person. There are also, unfortunately, times when precisely the opposite is true.

When Rockford stepped into the hospital, he was literally assailed by horrible, paralyzing memories of Peter's death. The lights were bright, giving the emergency area a white, garish glow. Loudspeaker voices droned in the background, paging doctors, making announcements. That particular hospital smell filled his nostrils, making him nauseated.

Valley Memorial was, by anyone's standards, an upscale, desirable hospital. It was spotless, well staffed, and architecturally pleasing. It didn't matter. To Rockford, it signified death, and loss and disaster. But he took a deep breath, pushing the barrage of memories away, and led his mother to the desk.

They were directed to a small waiting room, where they sat together, with Rockford holding his mother's hand. It was a while before a green-suited doctor appeared.

"He's alive, but unconscious. Apparently it was a stroke. It will take some time before we know the extent of the damage suffered. We are getting him stabilized and moving him to a private room. Then you may see him. I wish I had more definitive news for you both, but it just takes time."

Rockford nodded, and the doctor departed.

"He's alive," his mother whispered. "At least he's alive. There's still hope."

Rockford nodded again, horrified at the feelings and memories washing over him form Peter's death. *"Sorry, Mr. Rockford, but your friend is dead."* He had known it, of course, had known it the second it had occurred in the restaurant, but having it stated was a reality that had hit him long and hard. And his father? Alive and fighting.

Please, he prayed silently. *Let him live . . . and don't let*

him be involved in any way with Marco Slergetti and Pe-
ter's death.

Then he sat quietly next to his mother on the waiting-
room couch. Trying to ignore the hospital sounds and
smells, he tried thinking of the most invigorating and exciting and positive person he knew . . . Willow Blake.

"Can't put it off any longer. One of us must make the
call."

Rockford heard his mother's words, and knew precisely
what call she was discussing.

"I'll do it, Mother." She smiled gratefully, as he moved
to the phone.

George answered the phone on the first ring. "All right,
wise guy, what is going on? Why are you calling in the
middle of the night?"

He took a deep breath and told her what had happened.
He left out the fact that his father had been on the phone
when he had the stroke.

"Oh, no," George exclaimed. "I'll be right there. Gee,
I don't believe it. He's usually such a bull." Her voice
caught. "Hug Mother. Tell her I'll be right there. And
Rockford . . . is Willow with you?"

"Willow? No, I . . . uh, left her at her cottage earlier this
evening. Why?"

"It's strange. She had left a message here, sounding upset and frantic. I tried to call her back, but I can't find her.
She's not at her place, and the car is gone. I was hoping
maybe she was with you. . . . I'll be there soon." She hung
up.

Rockford felt his heart sink like a stone. Where was
Willow?

The doctor reappeared suddenly, motioning them to follow. "He's stirring. We're hoping maybe he'll regain consciousness soon." They followed him down the long bright

hallway, momentarily quiet, the only sound the tapping of their feet on the shiny linoleum floor.

They entered the ward, and were ushered into the private room. Rockford Harrison II was dwarfed in the bed, IVs implanted in his arm, oxygen mask in place, in a gray cotton hospital gown. Overhead, monitors blinked and beeped.

His father looked anonymous, vulnerable, helpless, surrounded by the white hospital bedding. Rockford swallowed hard as he looked at him.

Emotion welled up in him as he stood with his arm around his mother, watching his father's life signs recorded on the monitors. This was the strong man who had raised and guided him. They had not seen eye-to-eye on many issues. But never, he thought intensely, looking at the figure laying in the bed, could he have actually been involved with someone like Marco Slergetti.

There was a rustling sound as Rockford Harrison II moved his head back and forth suddenly on the pillow.

"I think he's coming to," gasped his mother, holding tight to Rockford's arm. "Oh, please, let him be coming to. . . ."

A monitor beeped loudly, and the doctor reappeared in the room. "So he's moving a bit? That's good. Let's see what we have here. He bent over the bedside. Mr. Rockford . . . Mr. Rockford. This is Dr. Donovan."

"Ohhh . . ." A soft moan escaped the sick man's lips. His eyes opened for a moment, and met those of his son, standing directly beside the bed. Recognition lit in them. "Ahh . . . getti . . . getti."

The eyes closed, and the patient stilled again.

"Well, that's a start," said the red-haired doctor with a sign. "Like I said, these things take time."

"I guess we should go and get some rest, and then meet George," his mother was thinking aloud.

"Good idea, Mother." He led her back to the lounge

and the comfortable couch. She curled up in the protection of his arm, cried a few tears, and then fell asleep.

Rockford sat still, staring at the clock as the seconds ticked by, feeling like a trapped animal, but determined to keep his head.

Where was Willow? The sentence echoed like a mantra in his head. Where was Willow? He thought of her warmness, her spunk, her determination. What had she done when he had left her? Was she okay?

Because he was definitely not. He had heard the muffled word his father had been trying to say in his moment of lucidness. He had looked right into those intelligent eyes, and had known that he was being given an important message.

"Slergetti." His father had been trying to say "Slergetti."

Fear rushed through his veins. His father had, in some way, been involved with the mobster. The mobster was nearby. And Willow was missing. He prayed with every tick of the hospital clock.

Chapter Twenty-one

Willow had returned to her cottage, but hadn't been able to sleep. Feelings in turmoil, she paced the small living room back and forth, trying to expunge the thoughts of Rockford Harrison from her mind. It didn't work.

How could it be? How could her heart have gotten so involved? A devastating feeling, almost like a physical pain, rushed through her, leaving her breathless. Was this what love was like? She had trusted Rockford, opened herself to him, with the unleashed enthusiasm that was so integral to her life. And trust didn't come easy for Willow Blake. Her father had ensured that with his instability and criticism.

Today, in her independent life, she shared her love with others. She loved giving. She loved Maggie, the children at the barn, the residents of the AIDS home, her coworkers in the real estate office. But she had never put herself in a position to trust again. Until Rockford. She had made the fatal mistake with Rockford. She had opened her heart, and he had let her fall. She had trusted the kind of man who did business with the likes of Marco Slergetti.

She knew she wasn't going to be able to sleep. She left the cottage, closing the door tightly behind her. She took the Miata for a ride, top down, letting the moonlight flow over her, and the wind cleanse her sad emotions. She drove for hours.

When she pulled back into the farm, she was still too restless to go to sleep.

She parked her car, and walked the short distance to the cottage, letting herself in to face her indignant cats. She fed them quickly, guilty for having neglected them earlier in the night. She stripped off her barn-smudged clothes, and gratefully stepped into the shower. The warm water cascaded over her, relaxing her tense muscles. She pulled on a well-worn sleep shirt, turned off the phone bell, and climbed into her bed, instantly surrounded by purring cats. Gratefully, her fatigue overtook her, her problems receded, and she sank into sleep.

George had just fallen into a restless sleep when the phone rang, and Rockford's voice gave her the sad news of their father's stroke.

It was only minutes before she was dressed again, and heading out the door. She left a note on her door to say she was going out of town, visualizing the panic that would descend upon the rectory if both she and the parish car disappeared in the darkness of night.

She had tried to call Willow several times that evening and had not found her at home. On her last call, she left a message giving the news about her father, and told her that both she and Rockford would be in New York, at the hospital.

"Is Willow with you?" she had asked Rockford, and he had been surprised at the question. So where was Willow? George pushed the little car as fast as she safely dared. When she reached the highway, she reached into her bag and pulled out the head covering from her little-worn habit.

There, she thought determinedly, pushing the speedometer another five miles per hour. *No self-respecting cop would give a nun on a mission a speeding ticket, right?*

The car sped away into the night, toward New York, and

her ailing father. She prayed all the way, even adding a prayer for Willow. At the end of the trip, she screeched into the hospital driveway, pulling the car right up to the door. She jumped out, and literally ran through the brightly lit reception area, punching the elevator buttons rapidly for the intensive care floor. If anyone had an unusual thought about a nun wearing a habit, along with the grungy gray sweat suit and some extremely used Adidas sneakers as she passed by, she didn't notice. She was going to see her father.

Chapter Twenty-two

Georgina found her brother and mother dozing on the couch in the hospital waiting room. Her heart contracted at the sight of her mother, face streaked with tears, as she sat protected by Rockford's arm around her shoulders.

"Mother . . . Rockford." They awakened immediately at the sound of her voice. After a hug, they led her down the hall to her father's intensive-care room.

Uncharacteristically subdued, George's tear-filled eyes regarded the man who was her father, the whiteness of the hospital sheets a sharp contrast to his dark peppery hair and sun-colored face. He looked smaller, lying in the bed.

This was her father, the man who could (and did) move mountains, who could bellow the house down, who could state his case in court with verve and vigor. An IV was attached to his arm, an oxygen mask covered the lower part of his face. He looked helpless. He looked vulnerable. The sight wrenched Georgina's heart.

How he would hate being so powerless! How he would resent being so dependent! She repeated the prayers she had said in her frantic journey. She sat quietly in a stiff vinyl chair next to the bed, and held his hand.

He had always been so "large" to her. With a huge presence, a loud voice, an unflagging determination, they had often been at odds when she was growing up. In many ways, she was exactly the opposite of him. Except the determination part. She smiled at the thought. She had taken

151

after her father in the determination department, that was for sure. But although he had questions, cajoled, and tried to manipulate her in her early years, he had accepted her calling to become a nun with a certain respect. He had never understood, but he had accepted her choice to live her life a different way, and she had loved him for that.

Rockford and his mother stood in the doorway, watching Georgina as she sat by her father's side. It was good to be surrounded by people you love at such a trying time. He felt a wave of need wash over him, wishing that Willow were beside him. His arms ached with missing her.

Finally, Georgina rose from her chair, leaving her father to sleep peacefully. As they stepped from the room, heading back toward the waiting area, she turned to Rockford.

"Where's Willow? I couldn't find her anywhere. But then, I hoped she was here with you."

Rockford felt his stomach coil with lightning speed. "What do you mean, you couldn't find her?" He thought of leaving her sleeping gently in the bed that they had shared so intimately.

"She wasn't at home. I called. She's not at her office . . . or at yours. I was worried. . . ."

Thoughts started racing through his mind—pictures of the burned farmhouse, Porter's office, Marco Slergetti's cruel face, Peter's bloody death, his father's muttered words. They were immersed in danger. Where was Willow?

Without a second's hesitation, he bounded to the pay phone in the hallway. He had to find her. He had to know that she was safe. He punched the numbers into the phone.

After the fourth frustrating ring, Willow's answering machine picked up. "Hi, This is Willow. Please leave a message at the tone. . . ."

He swore in frustration. "Willow," he said to the tape, trying to keep his voice sounding normal, "this is Rockford and I'm trying to find you. I'm—I'm not home. I had to rush to see my father. He's in the hospital with a stroke. My mother is here, and George. I'll call again later. I just wanted to make sure you're okay and to make sure you know. I love you. . . .''

He hung up the phone abruptly, surprised at the lump in his throat, the tingling in his fingertips. Where was Willow? He was momentarily overwhelmed at how much she had come to mean to him. He was going to have to find her.

He joined his mother and sister to find out the latest medical update on his father, feeling like he was being torn in two.

The medical news wasn't good. The stroke Rockford Harrison II had experienced had been a severe one, and it was possible that it would be quite a while before they could learn the full extent of its effects. Once he was alert again, his attitude would be crucial, needing to be as calm and positive as possible. They took turns sitting by his side, watching the proficient nurses and staff keep watch over his vital signs, sophisticated monitors beeping and flashing as the minutes passed.

At frequent intervals, Rockford attempted to call Willow, again leaving a message on her machine. As the sun rose and the morning clatter of the hospital increased with the new day, he called her office, only to find that no one had heard from her. His anxiety mounted.

When he had sent his mother and sister out for breakfast, sitting alone in the hospital room, his father began to stir. Startled, Rockford moved quickly to his side.

''It's Rockford,'' he said softly, holding his father's hand. His father's head moved slowly back and forth. ''It's okay, Dad. You're in the hospital. You're in good hands. Things will be fine.''

The older man stilled his restlessness, as if he could hear his son, but didn't open his eyes. Rockford felt his conflicting emotions dueling inside. This was his father . . . the man who had given him life, and who had given him so much. Could he also be responsible for taking so much away? But how was he involved with Marco Slergetti? Was he involved in Peter's death? The thought brought a bitter taste to his mouth.

His mind groped for an alternative, another explanation. But his jangled nerves wouldn't cooperate, and his mind was anything but clear. All that was apparent to him at the moment was that he was alone, saddled with questions with no easy answers. He felt like a rickety ship cast into a wild storm, with no anchor to keep him steady.

That was when he turned his tense face toward the doorway, where he sensed someone's presence. Willow Blake stood quietly, leaning against the doorjamb, not saying a word.

Maybe, he thought to himself, *my anchor has arrived.*

She couldn't help herself. After hearing the sound in Rockford's voice on the answering machine, she had to follow her instincts. Her rational mind was still angry and violated. She was suspicious of the broad-shouldered man sitting in the stiff hospital chair. But her irrational reaction, physical and deeply emotional, had propelled her to New York. It was a most unsettling realization. She loved this man, even if she didn't trust him.

Awaking in the morning, she had listened to the messages on her answering machine. Hearing Rockford's voice had done what miles of aimless driving hadn't accomplished. She had calmed down. His father had had a stroke. She could hear the vulnerability in his voice, the fear. She had wanted to be with him.

It hadn't been hard to locate the hospital. A few well-placed phone calls had given her the names of hospitals near his home. She had found the patient's location on the first try.

Packing a small bag without delay, and leaving a message for her office, Willow had steered the Miata toward New York and Rockford. She didn't stop to question whether she'd be welcome. She had only known that she had to go.

He stood from his chair with one swift, fluid movement, crossing the small hospital room with long strides. His long arms reached out and pulled her close. He buried his face in the softness of her windblown hair, smelling the sweet, fruity smell of her. Raspberry, he thought with a grateful sigh, absorbing the beauty of the nearness of her. Willow was safe and by his side.

"Ah, Willow," he breathed quietly.

"I'm so sorry about your father, Rockford. Is he going to be all right?"

Her eyes were filled with sincere concern. Having her in his arms made him feel both strong and vulnerable at the same time. With her body pressed close to his, he felt whole, invincible. But with her eyes showing she shared his pain, he felt safe to acknowledge the pain that was deep inside of him. He could feel his hands beginning to shake. He pulled her closer, her strength reinforcing him.

"They won't know for a while . . . it was a bad stroke. He came to once or twice, and tried to talk, but . . ."

"I hear these things take time, Rockford."

He took her to see his mother and Georgina then, while the nurses attended to his father. The time passed slowly.

"Wait and see." That was the basic diagnosis from the medical point of view.

"Wait and see." Was that also the diagnosis for her heart, her life? She watched the dark, strong man as he coped with the many things that needed to be settled for his father. He made her feel so good. Was it possible that he was involved with someone like Marco Slergetti? Would there be answers to her questions? Or would her heart be left in tatters if she trusted this instinct to love? *"Wait and see..."* Like a mantra, the words echoed in her troubled head, trapping her in that undesirable place between trust and doubt.

Chapter Twenty-three

The day stretched on, eventually changing to night, at least outside the hospital windows. Inside, with the bright fluorescent lights and the constant hum of activity, time seemed to have no boundaries.

The doctor brought the news that the vital signs had seemed to stabilize. Rockford's father, while not again gaining consciousness, was breathing steadily on his own. His pulse, his heart rate, his blood pressure were holding steady.

"It will be a matter of time," he told them in a caring yet professional voice. "As a family, you should conserve your energies."

Georgina had decided to stay with her mother for a few days, taking turns being with the elder Rockford.

Rockford would temporarily return home to Pennsylvania with Willow. He was torn with conflicting needs. He wasn't going to let her out of his sight, his fear of Slergetti well justified. But he couldn't bring himself to tell her what he suspected. How could he admit his naive stupidity? How could he admit that his own father had been involved in some way with the man who had ultimately been responsible for ending his best friend's life? And how could he tell her that Marco Slergetti had returned?

Willow followed his silver car in her Miata. Rockford wanted to stop by his parents' house for some more information before making the trip home. They drove through

157

the large wrought-iron gates that protected the Harrison estate. Her eyes grew large at the sight of the mansion. Groomed shrubberies, gleaming windowpanes, elegant architecture. Every sight said "wealth."

Willow swallowed a lump that had crept up into her throat. What would it have been like growing up in a place like this? It was the absolute opposite of her own experience. The hovel she had shared with her father had been decorated in "Early American rust." She had worked hard to believe in herself after growing up in that environment. But she had a feeling that it would be to even *find* yourself in a place like this.

She pulled her little car next to Rockford's in the drive, and unfolded her long legs to greet him. The knot was still in her throat. He looked so good. He meant so much. And yet, the echo of Slergetti's voice rattled in her brain, haunting her. She turned and looked at Rockford.

He, too, was staring at the big house, regarding it as if he had never seen it before. His handsome chiseled face looked at once forlorn. He turned, suddenly, and looked at her.

She met his troubled eyes, and felt her heart swell. This was Rockford. This was the man she loved. He would explain away the confusion and fear she was feeling. She opened her arms, and walked resolutely toward him, and he clutched her to his chest like a drowning man.

"Ah, Willow," he said softly, his breath rustling her hair. "I love you. I can't believe how good you feel right now. I need you so much. This thing with my father ... it's really got me upside down."

Her arms tightened around his neck as she hugged him back. "I'm here. I'm really sorry about your dad."

He nodded, not trusting his voice. He kissed her gently on the forehead. "I grew up here. I lived here for years. But right now, it seems so strange."

Thomas let them in. There were no messages.

Rockford showed her quickly around the house. It was gorgeous, inside and out. But Willow couldn't help feeling that something was missing. The house felt cold and impersonal.

He took her up the steps, stopping at a graceful pair of double white doors.

"This was my room." His voice was hushed, thoughtful. "The private domain of Rockford Farquahar Harrison III. He pushed the heavy doors, and they opened soundlessly.

It was a masculine suite, done in striking tones of brown and burgundy. The furniture was sleek and elegant, and not a speck of dust could be seen.

"Wow," Willow said softly. The room was a masterpiece . . . but it didn't look alive at all. It didn't look as if it had ever seen a moment of life.

"Pretty bad, huh?"

"Well, it's beautiful, of course. . . ."

"Go for the honesty, Willow. Your face gives you away, anyway." His face wore the trace of a smile.

"Well, I mean, did you actually *live* here? I mean, like write at that desk, and throw your clothes on the floor, stuff like that?"

He was grinning now. "Yes and no. I definitely wrote at the desk. I definitely didn't throw clothes on the floor. Georgina was the only one in this house who dared to do things like that."

"So you were the obedient type, huh?" A shadow passed over his face, the darkness was back. Yes, he had been the obedient type. Following directions, doing what was expected of him, without a thought of his own. And Peter was dead.

She saw the abrupt change in him and crossed the room quickly, wanted to feel his heartbeat next to hers again. He grasped at her, and she wanted nothing but to erase the look of pain in his eyes.

"Rockford," she said gently, burrowing her face into his neck. "Whatever your childhood was . . . that was then, and this is now. I learned that myself a long time ago. You're here now, Rockford. You're here with me."

"Yes, I'm here with you," he said in a low voice, thankful for the kindly, giving spirit of the woman he had come to love. She had put her arms around him, comforting him, and his emotions had surged so fiercely it almost took his breath away.

She pulled her head back suddenly, laughing, and started to climb up onto his high bed.

"Willow? Here? What are you doing?"

She stood up with a bounce, and took his hand and beckoned him to join her. Giddily, she started jumping up and down on the bed, like an errant child.

"Why? Isn't this your room? Don't you think it's about time you had a little fun here?"

Amazing himself, he climbed up onto the bed and started bouncing right along with her. Laughter bubbled up and spilled out from him, like a giant release from a pressure cooker.

They moved together until they collapsed, breathless and still laughing, as they clung to each other.

Rockford's heart swelled as he held Willow close, breathing in the smell of her, remembering her laugh. One thing was for certain—he would never look at this room the same way again.

The moon was high in the sky when they left the Harrison mansion to head for Pennsylvania. Rockford had spent time in his father's office, looking for any relevant information that would shed light on what had happened to him, but had found nothing. Giving Thomas instructions to contact him if anything occurred, and with a promise to return the following evening, Rockford and Willow departed.

He followed the little yellow Miata as they traveled, eager to get home to the peace and quiet of his apartment.

Things didn't go exactly as planned. The usually quiet street was illuminated in multicolored flashes from the two police cars that were strategically parked in front of the Victorian house.

"What's going on?" Rockford exclaimed, jumping from his car.

"What's happened?" echoed Willow.

"That's him," shouted a vaguely familiar voice from the porch. It was one of the detectives from the local precinct they had met when they had been investigating the Burdetts' truck.

Immediately they were surrounded. Two officers spun Rockford around, pulling his arms behind him, and slapping him into handcuffs.

"What the—" he shouted. "What's going on?"

"Get off him, you oaf," Willow yelled, pulling on one officer's arm.

"Stand back, Miss Blake." Detective Dunn appeared from the shadows, holding a white envelope. "You don't want to be more involved in this than you already are." He turned to Rockford. "You're under arrest, counselor. I have the warrant right here."

"Arrest? What are you talking about?"

"You're under arrest for the murder of your law partner, Mr. Porter Blank, who was found shot to death earlier today in his law office. His records had been rifled, but this was no random robbery. He had over fifty thousand dollars cash in his pocket, untouched. Your fingerprints were found all over the office, all over his files and phone, and the spare office keys which had been stolen, were just located in your apartment.'' He held up a plastic bag, and jingled the keys. ''You have a right to remain silent. You have a right to an attorney. . . .''

Chapter Twenty-four

The police cars pulled away quickly, lights now extinguished, leaving Willow standing alone on the sidewalk. She took a deep breath, and marched toward his apartment, her mind cranking into gear. She would have to call Georgina, and get help. Her attorney was going to need an attorney. She climbed the steps to Rockford and Georgina's apartment.

As logic replaced panic, she began to calm down. The charge was ridiculous, and would be quickly dropped, she was sure. After all, Rockford had been miles away in New York all day, witnessed by a zillion hospital personnel.

She hated to call George with more problems, but she took the news without skipping a beat.

"I'll get my uncle to take care of things, Willow. I'm sure he'll be out in a few hours. Call me if there's a problem, but I think it best if I stay here with my mother, who's determined to hold vigil over dad. No change."

"I'm so sorry, George."

"Well, I'm glad you're there for Rockford, Willow. He needs someone to believe in him, to trust him. There's something ugly and sinister going on there. We're going to have to warn him that Slergetti is involved in this somehow, and he's going to be shocked and upset."

Willow's stomach instantly felt like it was filled with angry bees. Rockford knew about Slergetti . . . he had even spoken to him. The bees increased their dance. How was

163

Rockford involved? She kept her unsettled thoughts to herself, not saying a word to George, while trust and fear whirled in a frenzy inside of her.

"I need a favor," George was saying. "Before you leave the apartment, can you collect the kittens and take them out to the farm? They've got to be fed and cared for while I'm away.

Willow agreed.

She gathered up the kittens somberly, getting them ready for their trip to her cottage. The silence in the apartment was deafening. All around her, the contents of the apartment were disturbed, evidence of the police search. Her head was starting to pound.

She knew, without a shadow of a doubt, that Rockford hadn't been personally responsible for Porter's death—but someone had. Someone had shot Porter Blank. That someone was probably named Marco Slergetti. And somehow, that evil man was connected to Rockford. She felt sick at the thought.

Ready to leave, she spotted Rockford's overturned checkbook on the floor. Automatically, she picked it up and placed it on his desk as she walked by. Three steps later, she froze, then backed up to see what her eye had glimpsed. It was a check stub for a check written three days before, and made out to CASH. The amount of the check had been $60,000.

The tiny flame of hope and trust that she had been fanning in her heart sputtered and died. What had Rockford done with sixty thousand in cash? If corpses could talk, she bet that Porter Blank would know the answer. And the police? They undoubtedly knew too.

She drove the car with the kittens on the seat beside her, their occasional screeches protesting their confinement in the small box. What was Rockford feeling about his confinement in a jail cell? Unwanted, but untamable tears began to flow freely down her cheeks.

In that instant, she knew how much she loved him. Totally and irrevocably. She also knew that she could never forgive or accept his involvement in the ugliness around them. Her principles were set in stone, and were as much a part of her as her skin, her organs, her heart. But her heart . . . it was as if her heart had been captured and catapulted into space to drift forever, alone.

When she arrived home and freed the frantic kittens, they skittered all over the cottage, being critically inspected by her own cats.

She was exhausted. It was after midnight. She had missed her last night's sleep at the hospital, and had been up frenetically cleaning the barn the night before.

"Don't worry," Rockford had said. Fat chance. But there was nothing she could do but wait.

She wrapped herself up in her much-used quilt and curled up in a ball on the couch. Instantly, she was ensconced in furry companions, both large and small. They nestled around her, and the gentle sounds of purrs filled the air.

"I have to think," she said out loud to herself. "But I'll just rest for a minute."

A minute was all it took for her to slip into a deep, desperately needed sleep.

It was a horrible dream. People were dying and missing, Rockford was calling for her, needing her, and she couldn't do anything to help him. She was tied up, and being slowly tortured with little needles—somewhere a hammer was banging, each blow exploding in her brain as a headache escalated to greater heights. She woke up.

She wasn't tied up, she was totally entangled in the blanket she had wrapped around herself on the couch. She was covered with . . . kittens. Little furry balls of hungry energy were flexing their tiny claws into any exposed skin they could find.

"Meow!"

"Scat!" She waved an arm and the tiny bodies jumped to the floor. "The U.S. government should hire you guys to do political torture with those claws. Take it easy. Breakfast in a minute."

She began unwrapping the blanket, trying to ignore her pounding head . . . and her stiff neck. And the hammering, which was still going on.

She jumped up, realizing that the pounding was real. Someone determined was at the door. She opened it cautiously.

Rockford stood there, filling the doorway. His eyes were dark and he look exhausted, his unshaven face shadowed, his clothes disheveled. Her heart leapt in her chest. Without a conscious thought, she threw herself into his arms, holding tight, feeling his heart beating strong in his chest, as he crushed her to him.

"Ah, Willow," he said softly into her hair. "You're safe."

"You're free. . . ." She nestled against the roughness of his shirt. As her mind cleared, and memory of her tortured resolutions returned, she pulled herself away, horrified at her treacherous attraction to him.

"What happened?"

"Well, the charges were dropped, as I was obviously out of town. But there were a lot of questions. An attorney dead . . . two people dead in an arson fire . . . two senior citizens missing . . . something very bad is going on around us."

His words were logical and caring, and his touch had a way of making her crazy. When they had been standing together, their bodies entwined, she felt like they were two halves of a whole. But the truth was . . . they were not. She knew. She knew he had been in contact with Slergetti. She knew he had written a check for $60,000 cash. She knew he had to be involved with the Burdetts' disappearance . . . with Porter Blank's death. Her mind was racing with a list of the facts, determined to keep her love-blinded body from reacting to his presence.

It made no difference that she loved him. He had left her and had gone to call Slergetti. She sighed in despair.

He pulled away from her enough to look deeply into her eyes, seeing her anguish. ''What is going on here, Willow?''

''You left me, Rockford. You snuck out and took off . . . You are involved with that Marco Slergetti in some way, and maybe in the rest of this. You haven't been honest with me. I don't know what to think.'' Her voice shook.

His face turned stony at the sound of Marco Slergetti's name. He did not deny her accusations.

''I left you because I had realized there was something I had to do, Willow. I didn't want to involve you, Willow. I wanted to find answers. I wanted to keep you safe. I thought you'd trust me, I thought I could trust *you*.''

The dark eyes were spearing her now. ''But you and I have some talking to do, Willow. It seems that when they found my fingerprints all over Porter's office, they also found another set of unfamiliar prints. They are yours, Wilhemina. When were you at Porter's desk, using his phone? And more important, why? How are *you* involved with Marco Slergetti?''

Willow felt as if a fist had clamped down over her heart.

''I am *not* involved with Marco Slergetti . . . but I do know how awful he is. And I know you've called him.''

''Stay out of this, Willow. This doesn't concern you.''

''According to you. But if he's got something to do with the Burdetts' disappearance, then it *does* concern me. They are my friends, and I feel responsible for whatever's happened to them."

"Stay out of it, Willow. Way out."

His voice was sharp, no sign of that fleeting illusion that Willow had been beginning to call love. She ignored the painful pounding of her broken heart. *Keep thinking, keep going,* she told herself. *No one really dies of a broken heart.*

Or so she hoped.

"I wish you'd trust me, Willow," he said in a low tone. "I wish you'd keep out of this. I don't want you anywhere near Slergetti."

Her eyes stung with unshed tears. She wouldn't let him see her cry.

"I'm sure," she said calmly, her head held high. "But I won't stay out of it. For anything. And if you think that I would, you don't know me at all."

"Don't know you? That's for sure. You turn your love and trust on and off like a water faucet. You change your emotions and commitments as easily as you change your clothes. Who's the real you, Willow Blake?"

She turned on her heel and headed for the door, her back ramrod straight. She would not let him see how much defying him cost her. She would not let him see her cry.

"Don't let the door hit you when you leave, buster," she snarled as she flew out of the cottage and climbed into her Miata with all the class she could muster. Her spinning tires left a trail of dust behind her.

Chapter Twenty-five

It was partly what he loved about her, Rockford realized in frustration, as he watched her drive away. She was proud, and strong, and stubborn, and independent . . . but right now those characteristics made him want to wring her neck.

After kissing her neck . . . He shook his head in frustration. She had no idea.

She had no idea of the evil that emanated from a man like Marco Slergetti. She had no idea how tightly and how treacherously his tentacles had wrapped around society. She had no idea of the number of lives he had wrecked, the number of lives he had controlled during his time as a crime lord. And he couldn't blame her. Even he, the high-profile defense attorney who had accumulated his court-room wins like notches on a football player's helmet, hadn't realized the danger of the fire he'd played with in the fateful Slergetti court case that had meant the end of his best friend's life.

Living the easy life, following directions, and assuming that he was always in the right, he had been somebody's pawn in a dangerous game. But whose pawn? Peter had been a casualty in that game, and he was determined to give the last breath in his body to be sure that Willow Blake wasn't the next. Whether she cared or not. Period. He loved her. Maybe he had never really loved anyone before, at least not with this intensity of feeling. But for better or worse, even if she ended up hating his guts, he would love her forever.

He stood at the sink and splashed cold water on his face, shocking himself alert, and rinsing away some of the gritty feeling from his overnight jailhouse stint. His jaw was unshaven and dark. It would have to wait.

He left the cottage at a slow but determined gait, his mind absorbed with planning his next step to protect Willow, and to unravel the mystery of what was going on. Willow would be glad, he thought with half a smile, that the door *had* actually hit him when he left.

Georgina Harrison had spent many a night sleeping in a chair. When her father's condition had stabilized, she had insisted that her mother be taken home to rest. She had determined that Rockford's release was imminent. Then, she had curled up in a little ball in the chair next to her father's bed, laying her head on the edge of the hospital mattress, and had gone to sleep.

Hushed nurses had come in and out of the room, tending to the elder Harrison's medical needs, and she had sensed their presence, resting the best she could as long as things seemed uneventful.

But her father's movement woke her instantly in the early dawn hours. His breathing had changed; she sensed his body had tensed.

"Dad," she said softly, her face right next to his. "It's Georgina. I'm here. It's going to be okay."

"No, no," he had whispered roughly. "Not okay. For Rockford."

She swallowed hard.

"Ok, Dad. I hear you. What about Rockford?"

He seemed agitated, his eyes looked wild as he tried to speak. Instinctively, she pushed the nurses' call button for help. She bent lower.

"Slerghetti," he whispered, his voice almost like a deep cry. Her heart wrenched at his effort. But he would not stop trying to speak.

"Closer, angel," he whispered, and she obeyed. She put her ear to his straining mouth and listened with growing horror as he spoke his next words. Then, exhausted, he closed his eyes.

She took his cool, dry hand in hers. "I heard you, Daddy. It will be okay. I'll take care of everything." Her voice was calm and reassuring, but inside, she was quaking.

The door of the hospital room swung open, and two nurses rushed in. "Mr. Harrison is awake," one called in an authoritative voice. "Get the doctor. Quickly." The other nurse disappeared with the swish of rubber soles on tile. "Sister George," the nurse continued, "we need to help your father now, if you'll excuse us."

George rose to her feet, then bent to place a kiss on her father's worried brow. "I'm going to find Rockford and Willow now, Daddy. Your job is to get better. Mother will be here soon."

He opened his eyes again, and looked pleadingly into hers. "Please," he whispered. "Save Rockford . . . and that Willow, and tell them I'm sorry."

The nurses took over, and Georgina left quickly, eyes burning, quietly saying a prayer for her father's recovery. And for Willow and Rockford's safety. And for her own courage and strength. "Angel," her father had called her, as he had since she was a precocious toddler. Well, she was not an angel, but she had a task ahead of her that would take a heavenly miracle to accomplish.

She gunned the engine of her car, and headed for Pennsylvania. She felt like they were going to be up against the devil himself, in the guise of one crazed mobster named Marco Slergetti. She just hoped she wasn't already too late.

* * *

Willow's head was throbbing and her nerves were jangled when she left the police station later in the day. She had been wrong. So totally and absolutely wrong that it made her heart ache. She had practically accused Rockford Farquahar Harrison III of being involved in the death of Porter Blank . . . of having a relationship with the dangerous Marco Slergetti . . . of having knowledge of the disappearance of the Burdetts.

And then she had stubbornly gone out to prove it . . . determined to prove to herself that she could rid herself of the overwhelming love she had for the man. She had wanted to prove that the instincts that drove her to love and trust him were in error. She had proved, instead, that he was innocent. She had proved that she was not deserving of his love. She had also proved to herself that she loved him beyond distraction, even though she had thrown his love away. It had not exactly been a good day.

The police had been more than helpful. Rockford had been removed from suspicion quickly. His information about Marco Slergetti had given the authorities a direction to begin searching. Slergetti's organization was disintegrating. He had returned to the country in a desperate attempt to minimize his losses and collect his assets before disappearing for good. Now that they knew who they were looking for, they were certain they would find him.

Unlike Willow, the police had been quick to see that Rockford was one of the good guys.

Everyone knew it. Even the newspapers. Today's headlines, which she hadn't seen until late in the day, had excitedly announced the discovery of the identity of the anonymous donor who had started the fund for the aids home with his donation of $60,000. Rockford Harrison was Ryerstown's hero, it seemed. And maybe her hero, too, except that he would never know it.

The Burdetts had been found. After fleeing town to get

away from Charley Morse, Mr. Burdett had suffered heart pains, and so had checked himself into a hospital in a nearby town under another name. He was feeling much better.

Her headache got worse. She turned into the long drive to the farm, distracted by her thoughts. Out of the corner of her eye, she caught a flash of shiny black through the trees near the barn. She quietly slowed the Miata and looked.

In the distance, at the side of the barn, she saw that two long black limos had pulled up out of sight of the road. Only the glint of sun off the shiny metal of the cars had caught her attention. Her pulse quickened. It was not a day for children's lessons. Who was at the barn? Her every instinct shouted danger.

She veered the Miata off the drive, and left it half hidden by undergrowth at the side of the driveway. She ran quickly through the trees toward the barn, skirting around to the far side where her arrival wouldn't be expected. She thought of the Burdetts. She thought of the vandalized Harris farmhouse. If something suspicious was happening here at Maggie's farm, she had every intention of stopping it, no matter what.

Rockford couldn't get rid of the anxiety he felt, burning like acid in the pit of his stomach. He ferociously pushed the gas pedal of the car to the floor, making the car lurch ahead.

"Warp speed isn't going to help," said Georgina from the seat beside him. "Better to get there in one piece."

He growled, but he slowed down. Georgina sat silently. They were heading out to the farm, where he was fervently hoping they would find Willow. His last thirty-six hours had been a nightmare, his suspicions about Marco confirmed, his father's stroke, his arrest for Porter's death, and the drama of the past few hours that he had spent with Georgina, finding out some unwelcome truths about his family. No sleep, a greasy fast-food meal, and a very real fear for Willow's safety had him on the edge.

She had spent a lot of time at the police station, he knew, and had learned about many of the facts that had been unraveled. But she didn't know it all. She had taken off for points unknown before Georgina had arrived to add the missing pieces of the puzzle, and she had no idea of what had happened since. He could only hope that she had headed home.

Marco Slergetti was a dangerous, cruel man, who would now be absolutely desperate and capable of destroying any obstacle that got in the way of his goals. And that included Willow.

Willow Blake. Did she have any idea how much she meant to him? Did she have any idea how much she frustrated him? He loved her with every cell in his body. He felt that she loved him, too. But Willow didn't trust love. Willow didn't really trust anybody. He thought of her . . . exciting, passionate, alive. Now that he had discovered the power of love, he ached to have her in his life. But could she ever love him totally? He had strong doubts, and that brought sadness rolling over him like storm clouds in a strong wind.

He couldn't make her trust him. But he would do anything in his power to keep her safe. First he had to find her. And then he had to stop Marco Slergetti. He had been responsible for setting him loose. He would be responsible for putting him behind bars. Visions of Peter and his blood-soaked tie viciously danced across his mind. Not Willow. He would not let anything happen to Willow.

His mind relived the recent scene at his law office—the police, the questions, his uncle. Georgina had come rushing into town with the information that their father had finally been able to give. He had discovered that his brother William had mob connections, and had been on Marco Slergetti's payroll. While Rockford's father, like Rockford himself, had taken and defended cases for people whose names had been linked to organized crime, it had been without any mob-type affiliations, hired to give the best defense possible as is promised in the judicial system, and making enormous fees.

But Rockford's father had discovered his brother's close relationship with Marco Slergetti, realizing that he and his son had been used as pawns, and that Peter's life had been lost in the process. The stress from his discovery had resulted in his stroke. Georgina's news had steered the local police toward William Harrison, who was now in custody, currently confessing everything to the police in the hopes of leniency for himself. But that, of course, left Marco exposed and desperate. He had little or no time to locate whatever he had already risked so much to find in Ryerstown before the police net closed.

Rockford looked across the car at Georgina. Her face was taut and worried, but determined. Her silence spoke volumes. She knew the danger.

They pulled into the farm driveway, stones skidding. His breath caught in his throat a few seconds later. He saw Willow's Miata pulled off the drive, abandoned in the trees. Where was she? His heart was pounding.

"Oh, no," whispered Georgina, and he followed her gaze. There, through the trees, he saw the two black limos beside the barn. His nightmare was coming true.

In a split second, George had dialed 911. "Tell Detective Dunn that Marco's at Higher Horizons Farm. Come quick."

"I've got to go help her," Rockford said in a low voice, "I can't wait for help." He halted the car and climbed out in one fast motion.

"I'm with you, big brother. Let's go." He turned to argue with her, to tell her to run to safety, but one look at her face showed him the futility of arguing.

"Thanks," he said softly, fear for Willow flowing with each pulse beat. They took off through the trees, in a run.

When Willow snuck up to the back of the barn, she found that only the bottom half of the back barn door was shut. She could hear Maggie's voice in the barn, strong and argumentative. She could also hear two low male voices, challenging and threatening. She silently opened the bottom of the door and slipped inside. The Burdetts' cow mooed softly when she saw her, but no one seemed to notice. She picked up a pitchfork that hung neatly on the side of the stall.

"You can coax and yell all you want, Mr. Big Stuff," stated Maggie firmly in her gravelly voice. "You aren't getting my farm while I have a breath in my body. Now get out of here."

The next voice that spoke was low and dripping with venom.

"Not a problem, horse lady. It makes no difference to me whether you have breath in your body or not. I don't have time for any more bungled farm purchases. I'm going to search this farm, and I don't have any time to waste with people getting in my way. Perhaps my associate can help convince you."

There was the sound of a scuffle, and Willow heard Maggie cry out. She stepped around the wall, into view of the interior of the main barn. A man dressed in black sat on a barrel, twirling a gun, smiling cruelly. Maggie was across the room, held tightly by a bigger man, stocky and tough looking. He held a gun to her head. They did not even suspect that anyone else had entered the barn.

Willow listened, assessing what to do.

"This is the last farm on this stupid road, so it has to be here. And I'm not leaving until I find it. Ice her, Paulo, then come to the house to help me check under these floors." He turned to leave the barn.

"You're a pathetic bully, Mr. Slergetti. No wonder you're such a failure. You sure don't impress me!" Maggie's voice was strong and proud.

Marco's face closed, his eyes almost slits. "No one talks to Marco Slergetti that way!"

Watch it, Maggie, Willow thought. *You're dealing with a viper here!*

"Get rid of her now," he growled to Paulo.

Panicking, Willow looked around the barn, searching for some way to change the odds of what was happening. But except for the animals, the barn was empty, and even the tools were carefully put away for the children's safety. Even the loft overhead was bare, accessible only by the long slanted ladder than leaned against its edge. Her heart was hammering.

It was the pitchfork against two guns. Willow didn't like the odds, but time was running out.

Feeling like she was playing a role in a bad western, she took five fast steps into the open area of the barn, ending right behind Marco Slergetti. She nudged him in the back with the pitchfork, and he stopped cold.

"Hold on there, Marco. Tell him to let the lady go."

He spun and faced her. She held the pitchfork steady, now aimed right at his stomach. He dropped his gun. His cohort froze.

But then, Marco's look of shock slowly changed to a sadistic grin. She had the sudden image of a lizard slithering out from under a rock, spying its prey.

"Why if it isn't the blond bombshell realtor. And you know my name. You keep showing up where you're not wanted. I told Charley to put you away a long time ago.

Unfortunately, he must have had a penchant for leggy blonds. But not anymore. People who disobey my orders do not have any more penchants, if you get my drift. And I don't have any particular penchant for blonds.''

"I'm hoping you have a penchant for the state pen, Mr. Slergetti. They will catch you, and you won't get off this time.''

"Certainly I will. I will have the excellent services of my dear Mr. Rockford Harrison, just as before. I've heard you two were an item, so you must know how it is. Mr. Rockford is my confidant . . . my knight in shining armor.''

Willow gave a sarcastic laugh. "Forget it, Marco,'' she said without a second's hesitation, looking into the mobster's evil eyes. "Rockford would sooner chew glass than be in cahoots with you again. You may have tricked him once, but not again. He has far too many principles for that.'' And as she spoke the words, she knew they were true.

"Oh well.'' He sighed melodramatically, turning away. "Paulo, shoot the horse woman . . . then this big-mouthed one, now.''

The stocky man, still holding Maggie, raised his gun again.

"Stop!'' yelled Willow, in a panic, brandishing the pitchfork. "Tell him to drop the gun, or I'll pin your hide to the wall of this barn.'' She pushed the pitchfork toward him, but he just laughed, not moving. But Paulo had frozen, curiously watching the young woman who stood up to Marco Slergetti.

Marco tapped his chest. "Bulletproof vest,'' he bragged. "Courtesy of one of New York City's not-so-finest. So poke away.''

It was her against two slime, one bulletproof vest and one gun, and Willow didn't feel optimistic, pulling back the pitchfork to aim for his leg.

But out of the corner of her eye, she saw a flash of movement in the back of the barn.

It was Rockford. She had never been so glad to see anyone in her life. Silently, in the sign language she had taught him, he signaled.

"Talk," he said with his hands. So she talked. And nonchalantly made the sign herself for Maggie's benefit.

"You know the cops are closing in on you. What is so important to keep you here? Just what are you looking for?"

"It's money. My money. And I'm not going to disappear without it. It's got to be here, this is the last farm on the road."

She saw Rockford motion again. "Talk." Then, "Look up."

"You want me to believe you have money hidden at one of these farms? And you don't even know which one? How stupid is that?"

He bristled.

"It was hidden . . . supposedly under the floorboards in a farmhouse. Unfortunately, the employee responsible can no longer be questioned as to it's location . . . unless you believe you can communicate with spirits from another world." He gave a nasty laugh.

"Well, it looks like you've bungled things again, Marco," drawled Maggie, without a trace of fear in her voice. "There's nothing hidden here on *my* farm, no matter what your flunkies have led you to believe."

"Shut up, horse woman. No one asked you."

But it was evident that her words had disturbed him. He was desperate.

Willow let her glance wander. Behind him, she could see that Rockford had positioned himself, ready for action. He was holding a heavy metal lid from a feed bin in front of him. Across the room, she could see that Maggie was tensed and ready. And then she looked up, and her heart caught in her throat.

High above their heads, a small, lithe figure had emerged from the shadows of the loft. It was Georgina. She stepped onto the long leaning ladder that led to the ground floor without making a sound. Like a graceful ballerina, she began to travel down it's slanted length, right behind Marco. A coil of rope was hanging around her neck.

Willow felt the sweat break out all over her body. Georgina was in plain sight of Paulo, if he moved his head at all to look up. And he had a gun. She swallowed hard.

But Maggie had seen her, and had assessed the problem. She began to squirm to escape his hold, instantly getting both Paulo's and Marco's attention.

"I told you to plug her, you idiot," Marco barked in frustration. He began to move toward her, then stopped as Willow thrust the pitchfork at his leg. He screamed.

The ruckus gave them the time they needed.

At that moment, Rockford had leapt from the shadows of the barn with a warrior's yell, his makeshift shield held high, as he charged Paulo and his gun. The gun exploded, and was deflected off the feed lid with a mighty ping. Maggie wrested herself free, as Rockford plowed into the stocky man with his metal shield. Paulo dropped like a stone as the heavy metal collided with his forehead, and Maggie grabbed his gun with a victorious laugh.

At the same time, Georgina was halfway down the ladder. She leapt through the air coming down on Marco's shoulders, as he fought off Willow and the pitchfork. He fell to the ground, groping for his dropped gun. Willow picked it up and held it on him, while Georgina deftly tied his hands behind his back. The sound of police sirens could be heard in the background.

When Detective Dunn stormed the barn with his men, he found the two culprits sitting on a bale of hay, Marco with hands tied securely behind his back, and Paulo holding his aching head.

Rockford stood with his arms around both Willow and Georgina as the police escorted the criminals to the police cars.

"I don't know how, but you did it," Dunn shook his head in wonder. "The world will sleep a little more securely with Marco Slergetti locked up in jail . . . as long as we can keep him there."

Rockford Harrison's voice echoed into the barn, low and strong. "Don't worry. This time, I'll make sure he stays there just as long as he deserves. It's the principle of the thing."

Chapter Twenty-six

It was several hours later when Rockford and Willow returned home to her cottage. To Willow, it felt like years since they had been here before . . . while waves of doubt and anger and confusion had filled the air. But now, many of the questions had been answered. Marco was in a jail cell, the Burdetts were safe and on their way home, Rockford's father was recuperating. But the major question remained, hanging heavily in her heart. What about the fledgling love that she and Rockford had shared? Had they extinguished the flame with their doubts and lack of trust?

She no longer had a single doubt about the depth of her love for him. And she would remember forever the feeling she had when she first saw him in the barn. She had met his eyes and she had known that she was not alone anymore. She had trusted that he would be able help her, that together they would find their way through the storm. But would it matter to him, that she had finally discovered trust?

The little cottage offered peace when they opened the door. Peace, along with the instant assault of tiny furry and finely clawed feet that rushed over them. The kittens were glad they were home.

He took her into his arms, still standing where they had entered, burrowing his face into her neck and sighing a breath of deep relief.

"I can't believe it's over," he said in amazement.

"When Georgina decided to do her circus performance and walk down that ladder, I thought I'd have a heart attack. My father will be amazed to hear about how all those years of ballet lessons paid off."

His face became intent.

"Willow, when I saw your abandoned car, and then those cars at the barn, I thought I had lost you."

"I'm not that easy to get rid of, Rockford," she said lightly, her heart hammering. "But I had my own doubts, until I looked up and saw you there. Ready to help me . . . I knew together we could do it. You were willing to risk running straight into a gun."

"I'd risk anything for you, don't you know that by now, crazy lady? I love you." His hold on her tightened, stirring fire-hot feelings inside, and she knew that her singing heart was safe.

"I love you, too, Rockford," she whispered, saying the words she knew would last forever.

He kissed her then, a deep, satisfying kiss that curled her toes and made her bones melt. The kiss promised a lifetime of love . . . until the kittens started climbing up their legs, begging for attention.

Laughing, they reluctantly broke away from each other.

"Feeding time at the zoo," exclaimed Rockford. I'll get the food, you gather the inmates."

"It's wonderful that the Burdetts will be returning and will be rebuilding their house. I'm glad the real estate and insurance details could be worked out.

She began scooping kittens from the floor, noticing the button on the answering machine blinking as she passed. She pushed the button.

"Well, hello, Willow!" the big voice on the tape filled the room. It was Mr. Reynolds. "We're back from the most exciting cruise in the world, and I can't wait to tell you about it. I stopped by the office, and things look like they've been running well. Although Mildred is acting a little unlike herself. She's changed her clothes and her hair. I'm not exactly sure what's gotten into her. I've decided that you both deserve a couple of days off, since I'm back to hold the fort. Do something exciting, and then on Monday I'll make you a cup of coffee on my new state-of-the-art coffeemaker!''

Laughing, and juggling four of the kittens, Willow headed for the little kitchen. The animals immediately attacked the waiting food.

"Reynolds sounds like a nice guy. Where's the other kitten?'' said Rockford, counting.

They began scrambling around the cottage, looking under furniture, in closets, behind doors. No kitten.

In the bedroom, however, the slight sound of a kitten meowing reached their ears. Puzzled, they searched for the origin of the sound. Far back in Willow's dark closet, they found a floorboard that had become dislodged.

Marco's words from the barn hung in the air. *"Hidden under the floorboards.''* Could it have been in the cottage, and not in the farmhouse? Flashlight in hand, they explored the area under the board and retrieved both a terrified kitten, and a square black metal box.

Warily, they opened it. It was filled with money. Neat stacks of large bills filled the box. A small black book sat on top. Rockford leafed through it.

"It's Marco's secret stash, of course. And a book filled with the ID numbers of several Swiss bank accounts. As well as names. Names the FBI will gratefully investigate, I'm sure.''

"Should we call them?''

"Not right now. Not on your life.'' He pulled her onto his lap. "I have other plans right now.'' He started kissing her neck.

"All that money." Willow sighed. "What will happen to it?"

"I have an idea." He laughed. "We'll turn it over to Sister George and let her deal with the FBI. If there is any chance of putting the money to good use, she'll wangle it out of them. Guaranteed. Not even the FBI can stand up to Sister George, believe me."

"I believe you!"

"She taught me how to do country line dancing, you know. I'm quite adept at two whole songs, if you want to give it a try some time. And I have the hat and boots." He chuckled.

"Sure thing. But I was thinking of something new. I found this group that is doing Scottish country dancing. It's lively and fun and you dress in costume and you could wear a—"

"A kilt?" he admonished. "You think you are going to get me into a kilt?"

She nodded. "You definitely have the legs for it."

"We'll see." They laughed. He kissed her again. "I love you, Willow. Forever."